At The Sign Of The Sugared Plum

Mary Hooper

BLOOMSBURY

For Pat Samuel
An inspiration to all
her friends

At The Sign Of
The Sugared Plum

First published in Great Britain in 2003 by Bloomsbury Publishing Plc
38 Soho Square, London, W1D 3HB

Copyright © Mary Hooper 2003
The moral right of the author has been asserted

A CIP catalogue record of this book is available from the British Library

ISBN 0 7475 6124 9

Printed in Great Britain by Clays Ltd, St Ives plc

3 5 7 9 10 8 6 4 2

Chapter One

The first week of June, 1665

'June 7th. The hottest day that ever I felt
in my life . . .'

To tell the truth, I was rather glad to get away from
Farmer Price and his rickety old cart. He made me
uneasy with his hog's breath and his red, sweaty face
and the way he'd suddenly bellow out laughing at
nothing at all. I was uneasy, too, about something
he'd said when I'd told him I was going to London to
join my sister Sarah in her shop.

'You be going to live in the City, Hannah?' he'd
asked, pushing his battered hat up over his forehead.
'Wouldn't think you'd want to go there.'

'Oh, but I do!' I'd said, for I'd been set on living in
London for as long as I could remember. 'I'm fair
desperate to reach the place.'

'Times like this . . . thought your sister would try
and keep you away.'

'No, she sent for me specially,' I'd said, puzzled.
'Her shop is doing well and she wants my help in
it. I'm to be trained in the art of making sweetmeats,'

I'd added.

'Sweetmeats is it?' He'd given one of his bellows. 'That's comfits for corpses, then!'

He left me in Southwarke on the south bank of the Thames, and I thanked him, slipped down from his cart and – remembering to take my bundle and basket from the back – began to walk down the crowded road towards London Bridge.

As the bridge came into view I stopped to draw breath, putting down my baggage but being careful to keep my things close by, for I'd been warned often enough about the thieving cutpurses and murderous villains who thronged the streets of London. I straightened my skirts and flounced out my petticoat to show off the creamy ruff of lace I'd sewn onto it – Sarah had told me that petticoats were now worn to be seen – then pushed down my hair to try and flatten it. This was difficult for, to my great vexation, it stuck out as curly as the tails of piglets and was flame red. Nothing I wore, be it hat, hood or cap, could contain it. I pulled my new white cap down tightly, however, and tied the ribbons into a tidy bow under my chin. I hoped I looked a pleasant and comely sight walking across into the city, and that no one would look at me and realise that I was a newly arrived country girl.

It was a hot day even though it was only the first of June, and all the hotter for me because I was wearing several layers of clothes. This wasn't because I'd misjudged the weather, more because I knew that whatever I didn't wear, I'd have to carry. I had on then: a cambric shift, two petticoats, a dark linsey-woolsey skirt and a linen blouse. Over these was a short jacket which had been embroidered by my mother, and a dark woollen shawl lay across my shoulders.

I'd been studying the people carefully as we'd neared the bridge, hoping that I might see my friend Abigail, who'd come from our village last year to be a maid in one of the big houses, and also hoping to see some great lady, a person of quality, so I could judge how well I stood against her regarding fashion. There was no sign of Abby, however, and most of the quality were in sedan chairs or carriages, with only the middling and poorer sort on foot. These folk were wearing a great variety of things: men were in tweedy country clothes, rough working worsteds or the severely cut suits and white collars of the Puritans, the women wearing everything from costly velvet down to poor rags that my mother would have scorned to use as polishing cloths for the pewter.

'That's a fine red wig you've got there, lass!' a young male voice said, and I realised that I'd paused beside a brewhouse.

I turned indignantly on the speaker. 'It's not a wig. It's my own hair!' I said to the two men – one young and one old – who were leaning against the wall, mugs of ale in their hands.

'And fine patches across your nose, too,' said the elder.

I opened my mouth to say more and then realised that the youth and man outside the Gown and Claret were making fun of me.

'They're not patches, William, they're called sun kisses!' the first said, and they both roared with laughter.

I picked up my basket, feeling my cheeks go pink. I

hated my hair, but even more than that I hated my freckles, and one of the first things I intended to do in London was to visit an apothecary and see what treatment the great ladies were using for their prevention. I pushed my nose into the air and moved on, only just avoiding a deep rut in the road full of all manner of foul-smelling muck. As I faltered, my foot slipped out of my wooden clog, but I regained my balance, picked up my skirts and carefully negotiated around the rut.

'Well danced, young miss!' called over the older man.

'It's a young red bantum fresh up from the country!' said the youth, and I pretended not to hear. At home I was always being teased about my vivid colouring but I hadn't thought I'd stand out in London, too.

'A spring chicken ripe for the plucking!'

'You mind a piece of old Cromwell up there don't fall on you!' the first went on.

'An eyeball or an ear!'

Before I could stop myself I'd glanced up to the over-arching gateway to London Bridge, where there was a collection of human heads pierced by poles, and let out a small shriek of horror.

I heard further mannish laughter behind me and was annoyed for being so green, for I'd known well enough that the heads of felons were displayed on the bridge – and I'd even been to a public execution – so it should have been nothing to me. The thought of a piece of one of those heads, though, one of those mouldered skulls, falling as I passed underneath – well, I forgave myself that shriek.

I walked on sniffing the air tentatively. London was

crowded and smelt foul. And not just farmhouse-foul, but a churning mixture of rotting meat, kitchen slops, boiled bones, sulphurous smoke and the sweat and discharge from a thousand animal and human bodies. The bridge was teeming with people because – unless you took a ferry – it was the only way you could get across from Southwarke into the City. I knew this because my sister Sarah had told me many times the route I should take to reach her in Crown and King Place, where she traded under the sign of the Sugared Plum.

It had been arranged a year or so back that if Sarah needed my help, and if mother could spare me at home, I'd come to London to work with her, and two months ago I'd been near overcome with excitement when a letter had arrived, a letter with my own name on it brought over by our church minister, saying Sarah's trade was increasing and that she would welcome me there as soon as possible.

'But you'll get lost in London, I know you will!' she'd said on that last visit home. 'You're such a cod's head you lose yourself going across the fields from home to church on a Sunday.'

'That's only because I don't want to get there,' I'd said. Why sit on a hard bench listening to a two-hour sermon when there were so many other, more interesting things to see and do on the way?

Our family home was in a small village called Chertsey which was a good half-day's journey away from the City, and if I could find things to interest me *there*, then you might imagine how I stared around me, marvelling, on London Bridge. There were a great variety of houses faced with brick, timber and all manner of coloured and decorated plasters, and they were of every shape and size, some crammed into minute spaces and others which towered and leaned this way and that. Even more interesting were the shops, and I peered, amazed, into the windows of those that were clustered along the parapet of the bridge. I had never seen such an array of things for sale in all my life: books, china, wooden toys, brooms, ribbons, wigs, buckles, pots, feathered hats and girdles – London had everything!

I began to plan what I'd buy when I was rich. We *would* be rich, I was sure – Sarah wouldn't have sent for me unless the shop was doing well. We weren't poor at home by any means – we had several fine chairs and settles, some pewter plates and space enough so that I only had to share a bed chamber with Anne, my younger sister (my little brothers had a room of their own) – but it was impossible there to follow the fashions. And besides, even if I could buy the silk jackets and flowered tabby waistcoats I craved, who would see me wearing them in the country, apart from booby gamekeepers or woodcutters' sons? In London, though, I might have the chance to make a good match – or at least be taken by a fine young man to a coffee house or one of the pleasure gardens.

Coming off the bridge I steadied myself as a great fat sow, grunting madly, and a litter of piglets swept by me and began rooting for nourishment in the mud and foul refuse outside a shop door. At home, mother always fed our pigs on the best scraps and leavings, but here I could see precious little that they could eat. Mother said that the tenderness of the bacon depended on the pigs being well fed, and Father sometimes remarked that they ate better than he did. The last time he'd said this, though, Mother had served him up a mess of muddy potato peelings on our best pewter, and he hadn't said it since.

I dawdled, sweating gently in the heat, staring at everything, listening to the cries of the street pedlars to 'Come buy!' a hundred different things, and wondering and exclaiming to myself by turn. So many busy, interesting people . . . what were they all doing? Where were they going? Two gallants passed swiftly on horseback in a blur of jewel-coloured velvets and gold lace, their spurs and stirrups glittering in the sunlight, then came several sedan chairs, then a bright yellow carriage drawn by four fine horses with gilded leather bridles. The carriage door had a family crest on it and at the window sat a lady dressed in rich silks, peering at the world over a mask held up to her face.

She was going to a romantic assignation, I was sure. I'd heard many tales of the court and the intrigues which went on, for it was said that the king had many mistresses and the gentlemen and ladies of the court not only approved of his carryings-on, but did the same thing. My mother and I had soaked up such rumours when they reached us through the ballads or the news-sheets sold us by street pedlars, but *now* I was set to hear them first hand.

Reaching the other side of the bridge, I turned right along a broad street and then paused at a water conduit in a small, paved area. The streets stretched out in seven directions here, like the spokes of a wheel, and Sarah had told me to go down the one which had a tavern called the Toad and Drum at the top. I did so, and found the street narrow and mean, with mud instead of cobbles underfoot. The houses were so tall here that rays of sunlight could only occasionally peep through the gaps between them, and their protruding bay windows meant that anyone living at the top could have put out a hand and touched a person in the room of the house opposite.

At the bottom of this street there was a series of alleys and I went down the first, past a dunghill and some piles of rotting refuse, and through into a small, busy market selling all manner of roots and herbs. Laid out here were rough trestle tables loaded with produce, and there were more traders selling from baskets or sacks on the ground. Food shops stood close by, their coloured signs announcing them in vividly-painted pictures and words to be: The House of Plum Pudding, The Gingerbread Man and the Pigeon Pie shop, and, being hungry, I started to wonder what Sarah would have prepared for supper.

I peered into the windows, then lingered by a stall selling strange, brightly-coloured fruit. I'd seen oranges and lemons before – I'd once saved to buy a lemon, Abigail having told me that it was most excellent at fading freckles – but most of the other vivid, oddly-shaped objects were new to me. I stopped, fascinated, amid the jostling people, but the shrill cries of the stallholders urging customers to, 'Come buy before night!' reminded me that I had to get on. If I got lost in the backstreets in the dark I knew for certain that I'd get my throat cut and never be seen again.

A little further on was another small square with a

number of ways leading off it and I stood there, perplexed, for a moment. Sarah had told me that the city was like a cony-warren and it surely was, although I'd had plenty of time since her last visit to go over the route in my mind. After some thought I went along an alleyway, passed more shops and entered the churchyard of St Olave's where I came across six small children standing amid the tombstones playing a game. One was evidently pretending to be the minister, for he had a long dark piece of cloth round his shoulders as a vestment and was proclaiming in a solemn voice. One was a corpse, lying 'dead' on the ground muffled in a winding sheet and the others – the mourners – were wailing and crying. I deduced they were playing at funerals and after staring at them for some moments – fascinated, for I'd never seen children play such a game at home – I stepped past the 'body' and went out of the back gate of the churchyard. Going across a small bridge over a river I took to be the Fleet, I finally found myself in Crown and King Place.

Excited now, I looked up at the swinging shop and house signs, searching for Sarah's. I saw the Black Boy, the Half Moon, the Oak Tree, the Miller's Daughter – and then, in a line of four or five shops, found the one I'd been looking for: a painted representation of a sugared plum. I swung my bundle of clothes over my shoulder and broke into a run, slipping and sliding on the cobbles in my effort to get there quickly, and thinking all the while how happy Sarah would be to see me.

Nearing the shop, seeing it close by, I have to own to a feeling of disappointment. From how she'd spoken of it I'd been imagining it to be large and painted in gay colours, like some of the shops on London Bridge, with a bowed window crammed with sweetmeats. It was not, though. It was like the others in the same row: small, with no glass in the front, and it had a wooden casement of the type that divided into two when the shop was open, the top forming an awning above and the bottom part making an open counter.

Sarah was in the back of the shop, chopping something on a marble slab and looking very cool in a cotton dress with a starched white apron over it. She was tall – as tall as Father, with a shapely figure, thick dark hair that I'd always envied, and no freckles. Not one.

I went in to greet her, sniffing in appreciation, for the shop smelt of spices and sugar water and its wooden floor was thick with strewing herbs, which was pleasant after some of the odious smells outside.

'Sarah!' I said. 'Here I am.'

She looked up at me and I was disconcerted to see that she seemed surprised – even shocked – at the sight of me. Surely she hadn't forgotten that I was coming?

'Hannah!' she said. 'How did you—'

'Just as we planned,' I said blithely. 'I took Farmer Price's cart to Southwarke and then walked from there. But what a muddle and a mess it all is in London. What stinks! What crowds!'

'But what are you *doing* here, Hannah?'

I put down my bundle and my basket. 'I've come to help you, of course – just as you asked. The Reverend Davies brought your letter to me and I was that excited – Father said *he's* never had a letter in his life.

But where is your living space? Where shall I sleep? Can I look round?'

'But I wrote to you again,' she said. 'I wrote two weeks back and said not to come.'

'*Not to come?*' I said in disbelief. 'Surely you didn't—'

'I wrote to you care of Reverend Davies again. Didn't he come to see you?'

I shook my head, upset and bitterly disappointed. I couldn't bear it if I had to go back to Chertsey! What about all my grand plans for living in London, for wearing the latest fashions, for attending playhouses and bear gardens, going to fairs and maybe meeting a handsome gallant?

'But why don't you want me here?' I asked. 'I'll be of such a help to you! Mother has given me some recipes for glazing of fruit and I'm much improved in my reading and writing. I'll be able to help you in all manner of things.' I couldn't understand why she didn't want me there and began to wonder what I had done in the past for which she might not, after all, have been able to forgive me. Accidentally tearing the new lace that she'd been making into a cap, perhaps, or running out of the house early on St Valentine's day in order to greet Chertsey's only comely young farmer before *she* did.

'It's not because I don't want you here, Hannah,' she said. 'It's because . . . well, haven't you heard?' She dropped her voice as she spoke.

'Heard what?'

'About . . . about the plague,' she said, looking round and shuddering slightly, as if the thing she was talking about was standing like a great and horrible brute behind her. 'The plague has broken out again in London.'

I breathed a sigh of relief. 'Oh, is *that* it!' I said. So it wasn't because of me or anything I'd done. 'Is that all? Why, there's always a plague somewhere and as long as it's not here – I mean, not right here—'

'Well, it's not in this parish,' she admitted. 'But there are some cases in St Giles – and a house has been shut up in Drury Lane.'

'Shut up?' I asked. 'What does that mean?'

'One of the people inside it – a woman – has the plague, and they've locked her up with her husband and children so it can't be spread abroad.'

'So there – it's all contained!' I said. 'And it's just one house, Sarah – we don't need to worry about *that*, do we? Doesn't a place like London have all the best doctors and apothecaries? I bet we're safer here than anywhere.'

'I don't know—'

'But I'm here now, Sarah. Don't send me back!' I pleaded, realising now that it must have been the plague that Farmer Price had alluded to in his strange expression. 'Oh, do let me stay!' I burst out. 'I can't bear it if I've got to go home.'

She sighed. 'I'm not sure.'

'I'll do everything you say,' I went on anxiously. 'I won't go anywhere I'm not supposed to. I'll be such a help to you, really I will—'

While I'd been pleading with her Sarah had been slowly looking me over from top to toe. Now, she shook her head. 'You look such a goose, Hannah! What a dog's dinner of clothes you're wearing – and why ever have you tied your cap so tightly about your head? Everyone leaves their ribbons dangling now, and that terrible old skirt – where did you get it?'

'The vicar's daughter,' I said, noting that Sarah's dress was of a pretty light blue with white collar and cuffs, and her cap was untied, its ribbons hanging loose. I frowned. 'Do I look so unfashionable, then?'

'As green as a country sprout!' said Sarah. She gave a sudden smile. 'But come and give me a hug and we'll close the shop early and go out and buy a venison pasty to celebrate your coming.'

'I can stay?' I asked joyfully.

She nodded. 'You can for the moment. But if the plague comes closer—'

'Oh, it won't!' I said. 'Everything is going to be perfectly fine.'

For so it really seemed.

Chapter Two

The second week of June

'Great fears of the Sickenesse here in the city, it being said that two or three houses are already shut up. God preserve us all.'

Sarah leaned over my shoulder to touch the sugar I'd been pounding for the sweetmeats we were preparing that day. She rubbed some grains of it between finger and thumb and shook her head. 'It must be finer than that,' she said. 'Like soft powder. When you've finished you should be able to sift it so that it falls like snow.'

I carried on pounding sugar in the pestle and mortar, keeping my sighs to myself. When, the day before, I'd complained about the amount of time and hard work it took to chip chunks off the sugar loaf and pound them, Sarah had retorted that if I didn't wish to work so hard I could take myself home again and return to my usual jobs of wiping the noses of our little brothers and minding the sheep on the common. So I wasn't going to say another word.

Sarah's shop sold all manner of comfits, candied flowers, and sugared plums, nuts and fruit. The shop had belonged to our Aunt Martha – mother's widowed sister – who'd gone to start a new life in Norwich with a farmer she'd met when he'd walked his five hundred turkeys from Norfolk to the livestock market in London. Mother and I had often talked about this, wondering who was the more footsore after their journey – the poor farmer or the weary turkeys – and if they'd driven him distracted on the way down by trotting off in all directions like wanton puppies.

Sarah was four years older than me. Anne and I were closer in age – there were only two years between us – and at home Sarah had been the grown-up sensible one who'd helped mother. She'd always been closest to Aunt Martha, who at one time had owned a little bakery shop in Chertsey, where Sarah had helped from the time she was ten. Sarah had a knack for making things. Mother said she made the tastiest gingerbread and crispest biscuits this side of heaven. She was good with figure work, too, and used to help Father with his accounts, even when it meant missing a dance on the village green or a visit to the travelling fair. When Anne and I used to tease her about not having a beau, she'd laugh and say getting married wasn't the only thing in the world and, anyway, she wasn't going to marry the first booby farmer who came along.

There were two rooms to the shop: the front one where the sweetmeats were prepared and sold, and the back one which was Sarah's living quarters, and now mine as well. There were two more rooms above us.

Sarah told me that a family had lived there until recently, but now it was just used as storage space by a local rope-maker. Our own living space held a small table and chairs, a chest of drawers for our possessions and an iron bed which Sarah and I shared. I'd asked Sarah to let me sleep nearest to the window, for from here I could sniff the fragrant rosemary bush just outside, which reminded me of the one by the back door of our cottage in Chertsey. I hadn't asked for this because I was homesick, it was just that London smelt so bad and was so smoky, grimy and grey even when the sun was shining, that sometimes I could not help but think of our pretty cottage with its straw-thatched roof and its door wreathed with roses and sweet honeysuckle. Alongside us was the old barn where Father made staves and spokes for his wheelwright's business, and in the garden were a great many neat rows of vegetables – so many that there was always spare to take to market – and our apple orchard which fair burst with fruit each October. Further off still was the village green with its cattle grazing peacefully around the pond, and the manor house, tavern and church. Chertsey was a whole world in miniature, Mother used to say, and she saw no reason why any of us should want to go running off to London.

That day Sarah and I were making candied rose petals, so that morning we'd risen at four o'clock to go to market. I was already quite awake by then, for I'd heard the first cheery call of the watchman – 'God give you good morrow, my masters! Nigh four o'clock and a fair morning!' – and needed little encouragement to rise.

We had gone to the flower market at Cheapside to buy pink and red roses and Sarah had bought six perfect blooms of each, first examining them carefully for signs of age, or bruising, or greenfly. 'Note carefully what I'm looking for, Hannah, for soon I'll be sending you to market on your own,' she'd said.

I'd watched her closely, of course, but my eyes had also been on the giggling maids buying armfuls of flowers: delphiniums, lupins, crimson roses and alabaster lilies to decorate the great houses. I looked for Abigail again, too, but with no luck. I watched the maids to see what they were wearing and how they behaved, envying them their confident manner and the way they traded glances and banter with the apprentice lads. I noticed one or two boys looking my way but I kept my head down, for I wanted to get rid of my freckles before I spoke to anyone. I was wearing my so-called best dress which was of plain brown linen and quite drab and hateful, but I'd undone the ribbons on my cap so that they hung loosely about my face, thinking that at least one part of me must be in fashion. Sarah had promised that as soon as we had time to spare she'd take me to the clothes market in Houndsditch, so I could have a new outfit. It would be less than a year old, she told me, for apparently as soon as any new mode from France reached our shores the great ladies – who would sooner be dead than out of fashion – would rush to order it, and have their servants sell at market any outfits purchased the previous season.

I carried on pounding the sugar, changing arms and trying to use my left hand as well as my right, and at last Sarah said it would do well enough.

'Now watch me,' she said, and she took a sharp knife, severed the head of the reddest, fullest rose, then carefully separated the petals, cutting any pieces of white (which she explained could be bitter) from the bottom of each. She told me to lay the petals side by side, touching them as little as possible, on white paper in a large shallow box. The same fate befell five more roses, until all their petals lay within boxes in long, perfect lines of pink and scarlet. Sarah then sprinkled them alternately with rose water and the finely sifted sugar and gave them to me.

'Put the boxes outside in full sunlight,' she instructed me, 'and turn the petals in two hours.'

Carefully holding the first box, I went into the yard at the back which we shared with three other shops. It was a tiny space, but Sarah said we were lucky in that we shared a privy here with just our near-neighbours instead of all the street. Just outside our back door was a rack of shelves which Sarah used to dry out flowers and sweetmeats at their various stages of preparation. There was room in the ground here, too, for a few herbs – one bush each of rosemary, sage and bay, which Sarah had brought as cuttings from home and had managed to root in the beaten-down soil.

I put the petals on the top shelf of the rack. 'Watch that it doesn't rain on them!' Sarah called through to me, but she was jesting, for it was a hot, dry day. The weather had been fine in London for six weeks, she'd told me, with not a drop of rain falling in all that time to cleanse the streets. Maybe, I thought, that was why it smelled so bad.

I pounded more sugar, and by the time I'd finished it to Sarah's satisfaction my arm and shoulder were aching fit to scream. I was allowed to stop so I could go out into the yard to turn the petals, and Sarah, after inspecting them, told me to sprinkle more rose water and sugar over them. The idea was to candy them to a crisp so that they'd retain their original colour and hue. 'Done properly, with enough care,' she said, 'they'll still look fresh at Christmas.' Then she added, 'Although they won't keep until then because they're so fragrant and delicious that they'll be eaten long before that.'

I sprinkled and sifted carefully. I tasted a small one, but it still seemed to be exactly what it was: a rose petal, reminding me of the ones I'd eaten with Anne as we'd played make-believe with our dolls, sitting outside our cottage with oak tree leaves as plates and acorns as cups.

When I'd finished dowsing the petals I lifted my face to the sun, happy to be outside. Then I remembered that more sun meant more freckles, so hastily pulled my cap lower over my forehead and vowed again that I would go to the apothecary the first chance I got.

Something brushed against my foot and I looked down to see Mew, one of the cats that seemed to come and go between our line of shops. There was a menagerie of cats around – tabby, ginger, grey, tortoiseshell, black and white – and I loved them all.

I picked up Mew and held her to my cheek. She was still quite a kitten and fluffy, with a soft grey coat like Tyb, our big grey cat at home. We'd had him since a kitten, too, and once Anne and I had dressed him up in a baby's gown that mother had discarded and taken him into the village wrapped in a shawl. When our neighbour, Mrs Tomalin, had asked to see him, saying she'd had no idea that our mother was with child again, we'd thrust the cat at her and run away home, cackling like chickens.

'Hannah!' Sarah called, breaking into my thoughts. 'Come in and serve this gentleman some sweetmeats, please.'

I hurried through into the shop, bobbing a curtsey before the man. He was wearing elegant satin breeches, an embroidered jacket and flounced shirt and was carrying a vast plumed hat under his arm. Taking all this in, I made another curtsey – a little deeper and longer – for I knew Sarah wanted to encourage such dandies into the shop. It was her ambition, she'd told me, to rise in fame and perhaps be asked to supply the Court with sweetmeats.

The man paused, his kid-gloved hand to his face, hesitating over crystallised rose petals or violets. 'Which taste would a lady prefer, do you think?' he asked me.

'The violets are very fine, sir,' I answered immediately, for although they both tasted exactly the same to me, the violets were more costly. 'They've been crystallised with pure loaf sugar,' I assured him.

He nodded. 'The violets, then.' He was wearing face patches and had a great flapping wig, but they did not detract from his lack of teeth, or the gums which showed pale pink and shiny as he smiled. 'Young Miss is fresh from the country, I'll be bound,' he said. 'Such fetching hair and skin is not often found in London.'

I didn't say anything but, flicking a glance at Sarah, saw that she wanted me to.

'Thank you, sir,' I said demurely.

'It would take a good many patches to cover those sweet freckles!' the fop went on.

'Indeed, sir,' I forced myself to smile back. 'Will there be anything else?' I weighed his violets and poured them into a twisted cone of paper. 'Sugared almonds? Herb comfits?'

He ignored these questions. 'And such hair as I've only seen before in the playhouse!'

I said nothing to this, just stood there, smiling as if I liked him, and eventually he produced a silk kerchief from his pocket and mopped his brow. 'It is most monstrous hot!' he complained.

'Perhaps some suckets – sugared orange or lemon?' I asked. 'Most refreshing on a hot day.'

He nodded again and the wig wobbled. 'Give me three of each,' he said, 'and some of your herb comfits, too.'

'Certainly, sir,' I said, raising my eyebrows at Sarah as I wrapped them. She took some coins from him and he turned to wink at me as he went out.

'That was the Honourable Francis du Maurier,' Sarah said, as we moved to watch his sauntering progress down the street. 'A real Jack-a-Dandy.'

I sniffed. 'A bumble-bee in a cow turd thinks himself a king.'

'Hannah!' she reproached me.

I giggled. 'Sorry. That's one of Abigail's favourite sayings.'

'Not now she's in service at a big house, I hope.'

As we watched, the 'Honourable' man hailed a sedan chair. As he climbed in, we noticed he had red leather heels to his shoes.

'Look at those!' Sarah said admiringly. 'He's been

here before but never bought as much.'

'See!' I said. 'I'm bringing you luck.'

'Maybe,' she said. 'And maybe we'll need it, for the Bills will be published later today.'

'What Bills?' I asked, puzzled.

'The Bills of Mortality,' she said. 'They list everyone who's died in the parishes of London in the past week so we can see what they've died of. We'll know then if the plague is taking hold.'

She sighed a little and her eyes darkened, so I thought it best to make light of the matter. 'What a long face,' I said to her cheerfully. 'Left to you, we'd all be in mourning weeds before supper!'

She did not respond to this banter, but simply turned away.

Later that day, Sarah gave me leave to go to an apothecary's shop. 'Although why you want to change your looks, I don't know,' she said. 'You saw how your colouring was admired by the Honourable Francis.'

'I don't wish for the sort of colouring he admires!' I said.

The nearest apothecary was Doctor da Silva at the sign of the Silver Globe, in the adjoining parish of St Mary at Hill. 'He's as honest a man as any,' Sarah said. 'I've used him for many cough remedies before now.'

I looked at her enquiringly. 'So they don't work, then?'

'How so?'

'You said *many* cough remedies. But if the first had worked you wouldn't have needed the others.'

'Get off with you, Miss Impudence!' she said, but she laughed as she said it and I felt she was glad that I had come to live with her.

I went out with instructions from her to buy caraway seeds from the apothecary, and some fresh milk from the first milkmaid I saw.

I took a long time getting to the Silver Globe, for there were many distractions along the way. The small shops next to us, six in a row, sold, in order: writing parchment, buttons, gloves, books, quill pens and hosiery, and I found it necessary to look into each one of them. Further along was a run-down tavern called The Tall Ship, a barber-surgeon's shop, some dark and mean alleys and a row of narrow houses with twisted chimneys, then another series of shops. Outside some of the houses women sat gossiping, or sewing, while at their feet children played with dolls or sticks, drew pictures in the dust, or teased their cats or dogs. Chickens pecked between the cobbled stones and occasionally a pig or goat came by to see if there was any food to be had.

The shop at the sign of the Silver Globe was large and wide, with bull's-eye glass windows. Inside, the space was deep and lit by candles, and its shelves were laden with all manner of fascinating objects. One wall held strangely-shaped roots and dried grasses, trugs of herbs, a huge egg – surely belonging to a dragon? – and baskets containing dried matter and layers of wood bark. On another wall differently-hued powders in glass phials were ranged, and there was a shelf full of ancient tomes and yellowing papers, and also a vast cupboard containing bulbous jars of coloured and distilled waters inscribed in a strange language. I took this to be Latin and could not decipher a word of it, for Latin was just for gentlemen to know, and the petty school in our village had merely covered reading and writing in our own language.

I was rather nervous on entering the shop, for I had heard that apothecaries could be sinister and powerful people, and I was half-expecting a man with a beast's head and a black cloak covered in signs of the heavens. But the young man weighing powders behind the counter had not either of these things. Instead, he had a comely, clean-shaven face with very dark eyes, and was neatly dressed in serge breeches with a white linen shirt and black velvet waistcoat.

'Good morning, madam,' he said with a merry smile which showed his even white teeth.

'Are you Doctor da Silva, the apothecary?' I asked rather timidly.

'No, indeed!' he said, laughing, and I felt myself blush. 'And if you knew the doctor you'd not mistake me for him.'

'Is he here?' I asked, feeling as foolish as a mutton chop, for now that my eyes were used to the dim light I could see that this fellow was only a year or two older than myself.

'He is not,' the boy said. 'But if you would care to state your requirements, I'll see if I can serve you.'

I now found myself in a dilemma, being too embarrassed to ask for a remedy against freckles from such a fine, good-looking lad. I therefore just asked him for the caraway seeds. While he weighed them up, he asked if I was new to the area and I said I was. I told him my name, and that I had come here to help Sarah in her shop.

He said his name was Tom, and that he knew our shop. 'And a mighty attraction you'll be to it too,' he added, making me blush again. 'Although it's a pity you've come to London at such a time.'

I hesitated. 'Are . . . are you talking about the plague?'

He nodded solemnly. 'The Bills for last week have just been published and the figures for St Giles Parish have doubled.'

'But there are no deaths in this parish?'

He shook his head. 'No deaths. But the doctor has heard of some cases in Lincolns Inn Fields, and some in Fleet Street, and he's gone to the Hall of Apothecaries now to discuss what's to be done. We will need to prepare some plague preventatives.'

'But perhaps it may not spread! Couldn't it just die out?'

He shrugged. 'The plague is said to go in twenty-year cycles – and it's almost that since the last big outbreak. Besides, there have been signs in the heavens.'

'Do you mean the flaming comet?' I asked, for even in Chertsey people had seen a comet which had flashed across the skies and left a trail of light in its wake.

He nodded. 'And last month there was a cloud formation showing an avenging angel holding aloft a sword. The people say that such a thing foretells a terrible disaster.'

I shivered, just a little. 'And do you think so, too?'

He gave a bow as he handed over my screw-paper full of seeds. 'I can hardly believe such a thing, Hannah, for according to Doctor da Silva, a cloud is just steam and vapour pushed into shapes by the wind.'

'So we are all right, then!' I said. I paid him, and he showed me to the door and opened it for me with a bow, just as if I were a real lady. I had other questions to ask but was so taken with his smiling dark eyes and the way he'd said my name, 'Hannah' – so softly, like a whispered breath – that they went out of my mind. Besides, I really didn't want to know any more about the plague. It sounded a fearful thing, but whatever I found out, I had no intention of going back to Chertsey.

Chapter Three

The third week of June

'The Sickenesse is got into our parish this week; and is got indeed everywhere, so that I begin to think of setting things in order . . .'

A few days later I contrived a reason to go to the apothecary's shop again. Sarah was making sugared almonds and was colouring the sugar syrup in pink, pale blue and green from the various tints she had. I suggested that pale gold almonds would look very well amongst these, and asked if I should go to Doctor da Silva's to buy saffron.

She looked at me and smiled. 'Saffron, is it? Or do you wish to make the acquaintance of young master Tom again?'

'That as well,' I said, for after I'd told Sarah about our meeting I'd thought of little else but him. At home there had been no one to think about – think about in *that* sort of way – so I'd had to be content with dreaming about impossible, faraway heroes like the king, whose image I'd seen on coins and portraits.

Now, though, I had a flesh-and-blood person I could close my eyes and think of before I went to sleep.

I put on a clean apron, changed my cap and rubbed the merest drop of pink colouring into my lips to redden them. However, to my great disappointment, I did not find Tom in the shop, but instead met the doctor himself. He wore black flowing robes, and was old, with a grey beard, knotted hair and bulbous nose. He looked solemn and wise, but kindly as well.

I explained who I was and said that I'd come for saffron. When I said it was for colouring, and not for cooking, he said the cheaper variety would do as well, and took a glass jar from a case. As he turned away from me to weigh out a quantity on some little gold scales, I took the opportunity (for I knew I would blush) to make bold enough to ask if Tom was nearby.

'He is not,' he said. He fumbled around in a pocket of his gown and placed some spectacles on his nose. Then he looked again at the scales and added a few more spidery stamens of saffron to the pile. 'I have sent Tom to High Holborn to see what measures the new French quack doctor is taking against the plague.'

I wanted to ask more but was nervous about what I might hear; also I was very much in awe of him. However, after a moment he turned to me and explained further himself, speaking rather scornfully. 'The Frenchman says he's discovered a method of preventing the visitation. He says he stopped the plague in Lyons and Paris.'

'And is that true?' I asked.

'Bah!' he shook his head. 'If any man could prevent the plague then he would become as rich as a king. And *this* is what the Frenchman seeks!' He spat on the floor. 'Frenchmen! They are good at nothing but being dancing masters.'

'Then nothing can stop the plague?' I asked, suddenly rather alarmed.

He looked at me gravely over his spectacles. 'We all have our preventatives and talismans, and sometimes they work and sometimes they don't. To my way of thinking, though, once that dread disease takes hold, be it on a person or a city, then it has to run its course.'

'Does this Frenchman make pills to take? Is it something you can eat?' I asked, thinking that I'd go there myself, right now, and buy whatever it was, for it surely couldn't hurt to try it.

The doctor shook his head. 'He has a method of smoking . . . of fuming out a house. A fire of sulphur is lit; sulphur and some other ingredients which the Frenchman keeps secret. It stinks the place out and – so he says – cleanses it of plague germs.' He spat again. 'The Lord Mayor of London has ordered that this method be tried. He must be in the man's pay.'

'And was there plague in the house that's being fumed?'

'Indeed there was,' he said gravely. 'Seven dead – the whole family – although the city authorities are not yet admitting that it was plague which carried them off. It will probably go down in the Bills of Mortality as fever, so as not to alarm the people.'

I, for one, was most certainly alarmed. Seven dead in a house!

Handing over the saffron and receiving his payment, the doctor then asked if there was anything else I desired. I thought about my freckles but decided

– in view of our previous conversation – that the matter was too trivial to speak of. I was surprised, then, when the doctor looked at me searchingly and said, 'Your complexion. I suppose you wish it to be pale?'

I nodded. 'Oh, I do!' I said eagerly. 'I've tried things myself – I've washed my face with May-dew, and bathed it with the juice of lemon, but nothing works.'

'What sign of the heavens were you born under?'

I shook my head, bemused. 'I do not know, sir.'

'I ask you because I use the methods of Nicholas Culpeper.'

I shook my head, not understanding. I had heard of this man and knew he was a herbalist, but did not know the methods of which Doctor da Silva was speaking.

'Culpeper decided that the planets in the heavens were responsible for the various diseases which afflict us, and that the planets also govern different parts of our bodies – our blood, skin, heart, and so on.'

I nodded, frowning with concentration.

'So to cure people he uses plants governed by planets which are in opposition to those associated with the parts of the body.'

I did not really understand, but I tried to memorise his words so that when I saw Tom again he would not think me totally ignorant of his chosen calling. The doctor asked my birth date and when I told him I was born on the 23rd day of July he said that it was no wonder I had fiery colouring, because I was a subject of the sun. He pulled out a drawer beneath his counter and showed me a long, papery-dry leaf. 'This is yellow dock,' he said. 'You must steep it in warm water and vinegar and leave it for three days, and then bathe your face with the resulting liquid.'

He wrapped the leaf in a fold of brown paper and, when I asked him what I owed, he said that Sarah was a good customer and I could have the leaf for nothing. After a moment's hesitation I asked if there was anything I could do to make my hair less red and less curly.

'You can comb it with a lead comb,' he said, 'I have heard that darkens the hair considerably.'

'Do you—?' I began, but he shook his head, staring at me over his glasses.

'I do not sell brushes, combs or complexion paints for the ladies. But if you wish your hair less curly, you may find that Lad's Love – a little of that plant in a herbal infusion – may help to straighten it, and you can find this herb at any wayside.'

I thanked him kindly for his advice, and for the leaf, curtseyed, and went to leave. On opening the door of the shop, though, I had to tussle with a great black-and-white hog which tried to push me back in. While I was engaged in pushing it out several chickens ran in, for there was a market at the end of the street that day and a greater variety of animals than usual were sniffing and grunting and trotting around outside. I caught two chickens but another ran towards the doctor, its claws skittering on the marble tiles, but the doctor roared at it so that it turned tail immediately and ran out squawking, its tawny feathers flying. I could not help but laugh.

Once outside in the street, I blinked against the strong sunlight. It was another very hot day and the air felt clammy. Smoke and fumes curled out of the leather tanners in the next street, a soap chandler was boiling stinking bones in a cauldron at the front of his shop and there was a disgusting smell coming from the piles of human refuse which had been scraped into a heap by the night-soil men.

The runaway hog had been claimed and was now being used as a pony by two of the children playing nearby. These two young boys, Dickon and Jacob, lived in an alley near us and often hung about our shop, hoping that (as occasionally happened) a comfit or two would turn out to be misshapen and either Sarah or I would throw it to them. They were about five or six years old and worked as errand boys, taking messages between shops and their customers, sweeping a path through the muck for well-to-do visitors or obtaining a sedan chair for people who wearied of shopping and wished for someone else's legs to carry them to their next appointment. They asked me if I would like a ride home on the hog and though I was tempted – in Chertsey I would have hitched up my petticoats and ridden him as if he were the king's nag – in London I was different, and I laughingly refused and went on.

Now I was out and once again surrounded by London life, by busy folk going about their business, all felt normal. Already the horror of the story the doctor had told me was receding. Seven were dead – but High Holborn was a way off, and possibly the plague would be stopped in its tracks by the efforts of the French doctor. Mother had always taught us never to worry about something before we had to.

When I got back to the shop, Sarah was weighing out a quantity of crystallised violets to a customer. As

I bobbed a curtsey to the young woman, she was speaking of how the violets revived her spirits and freshened her breath, and said that the ladies she worked with enjoyed them, too.

I looked at our customer with interest. She was dressed in a low-cut, primrose-yellow silk dress, ruched up all round the bottom (as was the latest fashion) to expose a yellow and red spotted petticoat. On her head was a little velvet cap embroidered all over with coloured beads, and under this – how I stared! – her hair was as red as mine.

She and I smiled at each other and it seemed to me that, as well as the hair, we matched each other in age as well. The pity was that I couldn't see whether she had freckles because she had some whitening on her face, and several black heart-shaped patches.

Sarah coughed. 'Will there be anything else?' she asked, and I glanced at her, wondering why she sounded so cold and remote.

'Not at all, thank you kindly!' the young lady said, seeming not to notice Sarah's tone. She paid, tucked the paper cone of violets into her yellow silk muff and went off, smiling at me again. She stood at the doorway of the shop for a moment, attracting stares and a murmur of appreciation from a passing gallant, all of which she ignored. Suddenly, she put her fingers in her mouth and gave a piercing whistle. A sedan chair came up, the door was opened for her and she got in and went off. As she climbed in the sedan I noticed that her shoes were spotted yellow and red to match her petticoat.

'Oh, who was *that*?' I asked Sarah breathlessly.

Sarah sniffed. 'That was Nelly Gwyn.'

'But who *is* she?'

'Well, she used to be an orange-seller at the playhouse, but now I believe she calls herself an actress.'

'An actress!' I'd heard, of course, that women and girls were appearing on the stage, but I'd never ever seen an actress before.

'You needn't sound so impressed,' Sarah said, 'for she's as common as kennel dirt. Her mother is famous for being drunk, and no one ever knew her father.'

'Well, whatever she is, she must be a very good actress to be able to afford clothes like that,' I said (and I spoke enviously, for I was still wearing cast-offs from the vicar's daughter).

'Oh, it's not acting that brings in the money,' Sarah said with an edge to her voice. 'It's something else.'

I looked at my sister. 'You mean . . . you mean she's a *whore*?' I said daringly – for although I'd already heard this word used several times in London, such language was forbidden to us in the country.

Sarah gave me the faintest of nods.

'I see,' I said. 'But anyway, she's very pretty. Can we go some time?' I asked suddenly. 'Can we go to a playhouse and see her?'

'Well,' Sarah said, and she frowned. 'I don't know that we should.'

'Oh, please!' I said. 'It's quite all right to go now – even polite company attend playhouses, don't they? Even the king goes!'

'It's not how it would look,' Sarah said, 'for we are known to so few people in London, that would hardly matter. No, I'm thinking of the plague. People are saying that you shouldn't attend any large gatherings, and the nobility are already leaving London for the country.'

'But there's nothing official, is there?' I said, and was glad that I'd not yet told her about the seven dead in High Holborn.

'We'll ask someone's advice,' Sarah said. 'We'll ask one of the clerks at the church whether it would be wise to attend a play at the moment.'

I said I would go to ask at St Dominic's, for I meant to couch my question to the clerk in such a way that his answer – the one I would bring back to Sarah – would allow us to attend. I very much wanted to see a play and, now that I'd met her, I especially wanted to see a play with Nelly Gwyn in it.

However, before I could go to the church – in fact, that very evening – a crier came round the streets. After ringing his bell so loudly that Mew fled into a box under the bed, he called that, by order of the Lord Mayor and because of the feared visitation of plague, all playhouses were to be shut up forthwith, and drinking hours in taverns were to be restricted.

I was bitterly disappointed, for I'd heard so much of what went on in the theatre – the shouting and singing and throwing of tomatoes by the groundlings if they did not approve, and of how the great ladies and gentlemen vied, like peacocks, to outdo each other in gaiety of dress. Now I'd have to wait until the scare was over before I could see it all.

And only Heaven knew when that would be, because the following Thursday, when the Bills of Mortality were published, it was found that there had been one hundred deaths of plague that week in London. And at this figure, the authorities declared that the plague had begun.

That afternoon Sarah sent me out for water. She gave me leave to take as long as I wished and make an outing of it, for we had stayed up late the previous night, working by candlelight to blanch and pound a goodly quantity of almonds to a fine powder, and she'd told me I had worked excellently and she couldn't think how she'd ever managed without me. While we'd worked we'd discussed the plague and told ourselves that it might not be as bad as people feared. For good or ill, however, Sarah could not send me back to Chertsey, because, as our neighbour in the parchment shop had told us, the magistrates were restricting travel out of London for fear that infection would spread to the provinces. This same neighbour, Mr Newbery, a short, stout man with a merry smile who loved nothing better than morbid gossip, had also said there was little hope of escape anyway, for if you had been chosen by the Grim Reaper then he would just come along with his scythe and cut you down.

I went to draw my water from Bell Courtyard. Although there were closer watering places, I favoured this one because it was a fine, paved area with trees and seats, and was much frequented by maids and apprentices from nearby houses. Also, the water there came from the New River and was judged to be pure.

The queue to draw water being quite long, I put down my bucket and enamel jug and waited patiently, looking around me at what the others were wearing (all were more fashionable than I) and wondering when Sarah would have time to take me to the clothes market.

As I waited, amused by a pedlar selling mousetraps with a monkey on his shoulder, there was a sudden burst of laughter from the front of the queue, and a hand waved madly.

'Hannah!' a girl's voice called. I saw to my great delight that it was my friend Abigail Palmer from home.

'There was no mistaking that hair!' she said, coming up and hugging me.

'Indeed not,' I said, for though I'd bought a lead comb and had been stroking it through my hair night and morning, it didn't seem to be making my curls any darker. My freckles, too, were just as bright and, as a result of the continual sunny days, now seemed to crowd across my nose and cheeks jostling for place.

Abigail had put on weight and it suited her. She was pretty, with dark curly hair which had sparks of copper in it, deep brown eyes and a curving mouth. She had on a black fustian dress cut up the front to show a lacy white petticoat, and looked very neat and comely.

'How long have you been in London?' she asked.

I told her, and said where I was living.

'And are you still in your position?' I asked.

She nodded. 'With Mr and Mrs Beauchurch.' She was about to say more when a cry came up from the front of the queue. 'Maid! Will you come to take your place?'

Abigail waved her hand. 'No, everyone can step up,' she said. 'I'll wait in line here with my friend.'

'And a pretty sight you will look,' the youth's voice replied. 'Two fair maids together!' The rest of the queue laughed, for a musical entertainment of the same name had recently been on at one of the playhouses.

Abigail blew a kiss to the youth who'd spoken, and linked her arm with mine. 'Now Hannah, tell me every piece of news from Chertsey, for I swear I have not heard a word of gossip from my mother or sisters since I came here.'

By the end of an hour, Abby – for that was how she was known in London – and I had caught up with everything that had happened to each other. I'd told her of the small goings-on in Chertsey, and about Sarah's shop and Nelly Gwyn coming in to buy sweetmeats, and I'd also told her about Tom, for though there was but a little to tell, Abby had a sweetheart herself and I didn't want to be thought backward.

We touched on the plague and she said that her master and mistress would have left the city already, except that eight weeks ago Mrs Beauchurch had given birth to a daughter and, due to childbed fever, was not yet strong enough to travel any distance.

'Do you think the plague will be really bad?' I asked.

She shrugged. 'It is bad every twenty years, they say. And I have seen some portents myself.'

'Which ones?'

'I saw the angel in the clouds with the flaming sword,' she said, and then she frowned. 'At least, they said that's what it was, though to tell the truth I could not make it out to be a figure at all. I have seen something else, though – the children playing at funerals. It seems that all over London they are play-acting the same thing.'

'I've seen them too!'

'Mr Beauchurch told us that children discern things because they are close to nature. They can foretell the future.'

I shivered. 'Pray it isn't so.'

Abby gave my arm a squeeze. 'Even if the plague does come, you and I are of healthy stock and as sound as 'roaches. We've nothing to fear!'

At home that night, Sarah and I stayed up late shelling and skinning more almonds while I told her all about Abby, and it was midnight before we went to bed, which was the latest I was ever up in my life. Just before we went to sleep we heard the night watchman on his rounds:

'Twelve o'clock
Look well to your lock,
Your fire and your light
And so good-night!'

Chapter Four

The last week of June

*'This day much against my will, I did in Drury Lane
see two or three houses marked with a red cross
upon the doors and "Lord have mercy Upon us"
writ there . . .'*

The gown being held aloft by the aged stallholder was
of pale green taffeta. It had full sleeves and a round
neck, the bodice was boned, had narrow tucks all
down the front and went into a point in the middle.
The skirt was set in pleats and its front edges were
drawn open to show a dark green silk lining and
matching ruffled under-skirt.

'Oh, this one!' I said, taking it from her and holding
it to me. I looked at my sister pleadingly. 'Please,
Sarah!'

It was Sunday morning and Sarah and I had already
walked the length of Houndsditch market where we
had easily sold both the vicar's daughter's skirt and
blouse and my own drab brown gown. With the
money from these I'd bought a dark blue cambric

dress, and Sarah had offered to advance my wages so I could have another.

'You'll find no lice or bugs in my clothes,' the toothless stallholder told us. 'This very elegant gown once belonged to a countess.'

Sarah didn't take any notice of this, though I was quite willing to believe it, for I liked the idea of having a dress that had been owned by someone titled.

'It's rather grand but it does look well on you,' Sarah said. 'The green suits your colouring.'

'It doesn't make my hair look more red, does it?' I asked anxiously, and Sarah assured me that it didn't.

'That gown is only two seasons old,' the old woman went on. 'The countess brings all her clothes for me to sell.'

'What else of hers do you have, then?' I asked.

The woman hesitated, then from an old trunk behind the stall she brought out a clover-pink velvet cloak with black silk lining and matching velvet hat with pink curled feathers.

'Oh!' I gasped, and I put out my hand to stroke the velvet. 'It is *most* beautiful. May I have this as well, Sarah?'

'Of course not!' my sister said. 'It's much too grand for the likes of us. And, anyway, it's far too warm at the moment for such a covering.'

'I could keep it until I needed it,' I said longingly, for it seemed to me that the pink velvet cloak was the finest and most beautiful thing I had ever seen in my life.

Sarah frowned. 'You wouldn't get the wear out of something like that. Besides, pink with your hair—' She shook her head at me and said no more.

I wondered afterwards whether she'd spoken about the colour of my hair just to put me off the cloak, but anyway, I settled on the green taffeta and was mighty pleased with it.

As we left the market a street-seller called to us, bidding us to buy her fresh gooseberry syllabub, and we did so, sharing a dish between us and finding it most refreshing, for it was again very hot. On the way home we also bought some gay coloured-paper parasols against the sun, and some new pattens to wear over our shoes. They made us seem very tall, but Sarah said they needed to, for when it rained the waste would wash along the street outside the shop to a depth of several inches. In view of their height, though, we decided to practise walking in them at home before we went out in them.

Throughout the trip to Houndsditch we had not seen nor heard one mention of the plague, apart from a poster on the door of the Green Dragon Tavern which read:

A most efficacious cordial against the plague may be obtained at the Green Dragon. The only true guard against infection at six pence a pint'.

Because we were in a happy mood, talking of home and our brothers and sisters, Sarah and I both affected not to see this notice.

Back in our room, I tried on the green dress, patted my curls down as much as possible and tied them back with a green ribbon. I then put a few drops of orange water behind my ears and, feeling very fine, my skirts rustling about me, I walked up and down outside the shop to take the air, hoping that someone might come along and see me. I suppose the 'someone' I was thinking about was Tom, but my friend Abby would have done nearly as well.

However, the only persons around whom I knew were young Jacob and Dickon, who engaged me in a game of gleek. This was easier played sitting on the ground, but as I was not willing to kneel on the dirt in my finery, I let Dickon play my turn for me. Pretty soon, a minister of the church came by and chastised us for playing a gambling game on a Sunday, and though the boys protested that we were not playing for tokens or money, he bade us put away the counters and act in a way which was more suited to the Lord's Day.

I went indoors a little later, musing on the fact that I had not been to a church service at all since coming to London. This was not because of a sudden turning away from the teachings, but because (and I must confess I was not displeased at this) there always seemed something else to do: cooking or cleaning, washing or repairing our clothes. And with the shop open all the other days of the week, there was only Sunday to do these things. Sarah told me it wasn't just us who did not keep the Lord's Day, for since King Charles had been restored to the throne in 1660, far fewer people went to church on a regular basis. The ministers blamed the king himself for this, for they said that he and his court were a byword for gaiety and freedom and did not set an example to the people by leading pious and godly lives as the nobility were supposed to do.

Indoors, I found Sarah was starting to make marchpane fruits. It was for this sweetmeat that we'd prepared all the almonds a day or so before and, as I was anxious to learn all the secrets of our trade, I changed out of my new gown and hung it in our room with a sheet over it against the dust.

The marchpane mixture was made by blending the ground almonds with sugar and rose water and dividing it into several portions. Each portion was then coloured by Sarah with either red, green, pink, or orange tinctures, and a little extra was made brown with cinnamon. Once divided, we took a portion each and stirred and pounded until it came together in a stiff dough.

The miniature fruits were to be strawberries, oranges, apples and plums, and Sarah took the utmost trouble with these, using a paring knife and other small instruments – which she said grand ladies used on their nails – to carve their shape. The strawberries were especially pleasing, being the rightful size and plump triangular shape with tiny indentations, as the fruit truly has, and a green leaf and stalk atop of them. I was allowed to make the apples on my own, and I did them green, with a dimple on top from which protruded a cinnamon-brown stalk. When the little fruits were completed Sarah instructed me to take a fine paint brush and give each apple a blush of pink on its side, then roll it in ground sugar.

To make the fairy fruits took us several hours altogether, but it was a most enjoyable task and, once finished, they looked pretty and delicate enough to tempt any passing elfin. We placed them on white paper and gave them another frosting of sugar before putting them in trays to harden slightly overnight and be ready for sale the following day.

*　*　*

The next morning I woke early to the usual cry of a milkmaid calling, 'Fresh milk! Fresh new milk!' and Sarah bade me take the jug to the door and buy some. After we'd drunk well of the foaming liquid – and Mew had her portion, too, with some bread in it left from the day before – we washed and dressed and tidied the shop ready for that day's trade.

At seven-thirty, as I opened up the shop, a town crier announced that certain Orders had been issued on behalf of the Lord Mayor and were being posted at every main water conduit and well. Every citizen was asked to take note of these and do as they commanded.

Sarah, who was arranging our marchpane fruits under muslin cloths to keep off the flies, looked at me in concern. 'That's sure to be news about the plague,' she said. 'Run and get some water and find out what it's about.'

I was pleased to do this, for I was wearing my new blue cambric dress and was mighty keen to give it an outing. Going to Bell Court I found Abby just about to leave there with a full pail and an enamel jug of water. She looked pleased to see me and put her containers down to give me a hearty kiss on the cheek.

'I've come up to read the Orders,' I said. 'What do they say?'

'Oh, 'tis just about the plague,' she said. 'Beggars must stay within their parish, and everyone is to water, sweep and cleanse the street in front of their door every morning and dispose of any slops in a clean manner ... 'tis not very interesting and just means more work for us maids.'

'But how is your mistress?' I asked.

'Middling well,' Abby said. Her face brightened. 'But she has bid me go to the Exchange tomorrow morning on an errand. Why don't you ask your sister if you can have leave to go, and we can meet up.'

'Where's that?' I asked, puzzled.

'You goose!' she said. 'Have you not heard of the Royal Exchange? 'Tis the most fashionable meeting place in the city! At least, it is apart from the coffee houses – and no decent girl would be seen in one of those without a gentleman.'

I tried to cover my ignorance by assuring her that I had heard of the Royal Exchange, but wanted to know exactly where it was.

''Tis at Cornhill. But I'll meet you here about midday.'

I said I would do my best to be there, and went to read the Orders, which were just a list of rules and instructions for the prevention of further contagion. They included directions for medicines to be prescribed against the sickness – different ones according to whether you were rich or poor – the banning of all needless gatherings of people and a ruling that beggars must not be allowed to go about from parish to parish in case this spread the disease.

Several folk were gathered about the poster and many of them, not being readers, begged me to impart its contents. As more people arrived I was asked to do this several times over, until I almost knew the words off by heart. As I read them once again it came to me that those who surrounded me did not seem overly worried about them. They made good-humoured comments about the contents, laughing and saying it would be more work for death-mongering coffin makers, and naming doctors and apothecaries as quacks and charlatans.

'They would as soon kill you as cure you – for they get paid either way,' one woman said to me cheerfully, and again I could not bring myself to believe that these Orders – this plague – was any great matter. The sun was shining, the day was fair and the people around me were bonny and of good heart. Perhaps the authorities had just been thrown into a panic by a few deaths.

Returning home, however, I was given some cause to change my mind, for I blundered unawares into the very heart of the dread plague-land. Going the long way back – for I was trying to make my journey lead me past Doctor da Silva's shop – I found myself approaching the parish of St Giles. Sarah had told me this was a disreputable area and that many derelicts and paupers had made their homes amongst its slums. It being daylight, however, and the streets being busy, I did not worry about entering. As I ventured further into the mean and shabby streets though, I began to feel considerable unease, for in some passageways shops were closed up and there were few people about, almost as if it was a holy day. I pressed on, for though I had never been this way before, being a country girl I knew by the position of the sun in the sky that I was going in the right direction.

After a few moments I reached Cock and Ball Alley and judged I should turn left into it. But a man lounging by the first house held his hand up to bar my way. He held a sharpened halberd aloft and was a dirty and ugly-looking fellow with a red, sweaty face and several teeth missing at the front.

'I need to get along here,' I said, somewhat nervously.

'No, you don't,' he said, and he pointed to the door of the house behind him.

This was a stout oak door, cast all about with heavy chains and locks, and as I stared at it my heart seemed to contract, for it had a great painted red cross on it and a written notice saying: LORD, HAVE MERCY ON US.

I gasped, my stomach lurching. I knew already, of course, what these signs meant, but the ill-favoured fellow was eager to explain further. 'Four dead of plague in there and the rest shut up for forty days!' he said. He pointed with his halberd. 'And further down Cock and Ball Alley two more houses are enclosed.'

I stared up at the house before me. One small window was open on the second floor, but apart from that it was shuttered and silent.

'But . . . but how do they eat? Who gets their provisions?' I asked.

'I does their errands,' the fellow said, 'and buys their milk and bread.'

'But how do they get on, shut up all that time? How do they take the air?'

'They don't take no air,' he said. 'The only time that door will be opened is to bring out a body.' He scratched his head and I saw something – some small insect – dart along his greasy scalp. 'Four dead so far and two more expected before nightfall.'

As I stood there, horrified, staring at the shuttered windows and trying to imagine how the people fared inside the house, there came from within a sudden wailing, turning to a high-pitched scream which went on and on without any end. There was the sound of running feet and another scream joined the first.

I stared at the man waiting for confirmation, for I was rooted to the spot and felt unable to leave until I knew the worst. He looked at me and shrugged. ''Tis another,' was all he said.

A woman walking by us on the other side of the road crossed herself and hurried away. As several others gathered outside a shop and spoke together, looking with frightened eyes towards the house, I began to back away, going home the way I'd arrived, getting out of St Giles with all haste. Before I'd got very far, I heard the bells of the parish church, tolling mournfully to tell of that latest death.

Chapter Five

The first week of July

'Asking how the Plague goes, the Parish Clerk tells me that it increases much, and much in our Parish . . .'

Sarah, being pleased with the way I was working, gave me permission to take an excursion with Abby, and the following day we met at midday as planned.

'Well, the plague cannot be that far advanced,' said Abby as we walked through the vast stone pillars into the Royal Exchange, 'for the king and his courtiers are still in London. They would surely have left if there was any chance of the pestilence coming near to his royal person.'

I shrugged, not knowing the answer to this.

Abby lowered her voice. 'Although I've heard that the royal person is not that fussy about who he *does* get near. The likes of actresses and whores . . .' Here she paused and we looked at each other gleefully. '. . . have had bastard children by him.'

'Have they really?' I said, and I would have asked more except that I was entranced and amazed and distracted on all sides by the scene before me.

The Royal Exchange was a great blackened stone building, open in the centre, with a gallery around each of its two floors. Small, alluring, candlelit shops lined these galleries, each with its own bright metal sign hanging over its doorway proclaiming its wares. Groups of young men gathered in the centre court, looking intently at the women who passed – who, in turn, affected not to see them at all. Occasionally, I heard a long low whistle or a comment of, 'By gad!' or 'Look at that filly!'

I tried to memorise what people were wearing to tell Sarah later, for it seemed to me that each group was more dazzling and brilliantly dressed than the one before. The men were mostly in velvet breeches in rich colours, gartered in gold at the knee, with handsome thigh-length black coats which bore silver-and-gold embroidered cuffs. Some carried swords or three-cornered hats with vast plumes, and some had short periwigs. The very finest wore elaborate curling wigs and their faces were powdered and patched almost as carefully as those of the women.

The women themselves were like birds of paradise in summer gowns made of lace, spangled satin, muslin or watered moiré in all colours of the rainbow: jade green, palest ivory, rich plum, lavender and dusky pink. Most of them had tumbling blonde hair (all false, Abby said in a whisper) and their whitened skin contrasted greatly with their dark eyebrows and sweeping lashes. Their bodices were low – so low, in fact, that it was a wonder that their voluptuous bosoms did not spill out of their gowns – and most carried elaborate, feather-loaded fans. Those who did not affect to hide behind their fans were wearing vizards or masks, held up to their faces on sticks.

It was difficult not to gawp, and in the end Abby had to tug my arm to make me move. 'Do come on, Hannah,' she hissed. 'You're staring about you like a country bridegroom at a whorehouse.'

'Sorry,' I murmured, for my sights had just been engaged by a woman wearing a striking bright fuschia-pink dress with pearl-grey under-skirt and the largest, most ludicrous headdress of flowers and dressed hair I had ever seen. She was an old woman, at least sixty, and her face and upper body were painted waxy-white and covered in black, spangled patches. Her lips were blood red and her eyebrows painted on in large semi-hoops, giving her a permanent expression of surprise.

'Who *is* she?' I asked Abby in a low voice. 'Someone's mistress?'

Abby looked where I was staring and shuddered. 'Years ago, maybe,' she said. 'And now she wears whitening and patches to hide the wrinkles and pox marks. Pray God you and I find good husbands who live long, Hannah, for I would not like to be on the market again at her age.' She tugged my arm. 'Come on, I have to get some silver ribbons for Madam. She's feeling a little better and has a fancy to bedeck herself.' She stepped confidently towards one of the small shops and I scuttled behind her, my eyes darting everywhere.

The little shops sold a thousand varieties of luxurious things: tortoiseshell boxes, silver comfit holders, velvet capes, soft leather gloves, jewelled bags, satin petticoats, watches and clocks, masks, birdcages, linen handkerchiefs and every possible item of haberdashery. The one thing I did not see was a confectioners, and I immediately began to dream of having a shop here, of me and Sarah being at the Royal Exchange, our Sugared Plum sign hanging here amongst the glittering signs of so many others.

Abby made her purchase and, very reluctantly, we set off for home, but not before we'd taken a turn of the inner court once again and seen a most beautiful, very elegant tall woman in flame-coloured silk whom Abby said was Barbara Castlemaine, the king's mistress. I was able to see little more than this lady's head and fine shoulders, however, because a small crowd of gallants were surrounding her, each, it seemed, trying to outdo the others in swaggers and elaborate courtly gestures.

I left Abby at Belle Vue, the house where she was in service. It was a handsome five-storey dwelling set in a cobbled and flowered courtyard, with stables alongside, and Abby promised that the next time the master and mistress were out, she would show me around it. 'We'll be quite safe,' she said, 'for the cook spends her afternoons drinking and playing cards with the grooms and the housekeeper has a lover and is never here. When Mr Beauchurch is out and the mistress is asleep I have free run of the house.' She eyed me quizzically. 'But talking of lovers . . . you have not spoken of your beau. Tom, isn't it?'

I blushed. 'Really, I hardly know him,' I had to confess to her.

'Is that so?'

'Although, if knowing him could be advanced by thinking of him, then I own I know him well enough to marry him!' I said.

She laughed. 'You'll have to contrive another meeting. 'Tis easily done. My sweetheart is 'prenticed to a bookbinder and I find all sorts of excuses and reasons to go in and question him on the book business, although I find it horribly dreary.'

I said I would think of something, and see her soon, then we kissed and parted.

When I got home, I told Sarah in great detail everything I'd seen at the Exchange, and also assured her that I was determined that one day we would have a shop there.

She was in a happy mood and joined in, saying that we might easily do that — for she had done well that day and almost sold out of our fairy fruit. 'Everyone who passed admired it,' she said, 'and several ladies said they would tell their friends about us. There is just one thing—'

'What's that?' I asked absently, my mind still on all the things I'd seen.

'We must close the shop early this afternoon and set to making some more,' she said.

Inwardly, I groaned a little, thinking of the cracking of the almond shells and the laborious peeling and pounding of the nut kernels, but did not say a word.

That evening, while Sarah and I were still grinding nuts, the crier came to say that because of fear of the dread visitation, that very day the king and his courtiers were leaving London for Isleworth. Meanwhile, to try to avert the sickness, his people were ordered to take to the churches and observe some days of fasting and solemn prayer, the first of which was to be the following Wednesday. On this day all shops, markets and taverns were to be closed and everyone was to attend church at least once. Hearing this, I immediately thought of Tom and what a chance it was to see him – for I would make sure to attend the church in his parish as well as ours – and how fine I would look in my new green dress with its matching petticoat.

When, though, three days later, the new Bill of Mortality was published with the news that across London, five hundred persons had died of the plague in that first week of July, I upbraided myself for my vanity and made a silent promise that I would attend church as devoutly and sincerely as a nun, and not give another thought to how I looked that day.

I did not see Tom at church, and indeed it was a most grave and seemingly never-ending sermon in St Mary at Hill, so that I was mighty sorry I had decided to attend it and not go back to the shop with Sarah after the service at St Dominic's. The vicar there wore a rough woollen shirt and had ashes on his forehead, and he roared from the pulpit that if the plague struck in its full terror, then we were all to blame by our corrupt behaviour. He said that if we wanted to avert the full might of it then we must change our sinful ways.

I looked round at my fellow men, wondering what they had to confess and thinking that they must all have souls as black as those of heathens if the vicar was right. Try as I might, however, I could not think of a single really bad thing of my own to confess. There was vanity, of course, but I had quite given up on my freckles and was almost resolved to live with them, and could such a seemingly small thing like wishing to have darker hair and finer gowns really bring down the wrath of God on us?

That afternoon, while we were supposed to be fasting in silent contemplation of our fate (in reality, partaking of bread and cheese and talking of home) there came a tap on the door of the shop.

Going through, I was disconcerted to find Tom standing there and, moreover, Tom in Sunday best starched shirt and red fustian breeches, a felt hat on his head.

He gave me a slight bow, his eyes raking my face and smiling, and bade me good day. I curtsied and bade him the same, but then I was stuck and did not know what was the correct thing to do. At home in Chertsey I would have invited him in to take some small beer, but here in London I did not know if it was appropriate. Sarah, though, seeming to sense I was at a loss, called to me.

'Don't leave Master Tom standing on the doorstep like a boot scraper,' was what she said, and it made him laugh. He tugged off his hat as he came through to our back room, and his eyes fell on Mew. I had tied an old ribbon around her neck and she was rolling across the floor playing with the fraying edge of it. 'Oh, haven't you heard?' he exclaimed.

I looked down at Mew in some concern. I feared that he was going to say that Mew belonged to someone important and was being sought by them, for I'd grown very fond of the kitten and would not have liked to give her up.

'Heard what?' Sarah asked.

'By order of the Lord Mayor all the cats and

dogs . . .' He hesitated. 'All cats and dogs are to be killed.'

Sarah and I both gasped, and I picked up Mew immediately and held her tight.

'Why?' we both asked together.

'They think the sickness may be caused by cats and dogs running abroad and spreading it to different houses. Doctor da Silva does not believe this is possible, but . . .' he shrugged, 'this is what the authorities say. There are carts going round and the drivers are being paid two pence for the body of each dog or cat they club to death and bring in.'

I gave a little scream.

'Is that really true, Tom?' Sarah asked. 'You would not joke with us?'

'Indeed not!' Tom said. 'I can see how fond you are of the little thing.' He put out his hand to stroke Mew's soft fur. 'All is not lost,' he said, 'for if you keep kitty inside they won't see her. The men have no authority to come into the house and club the animals there – although in view of the bounty being paid, some no doubt will try to do so.'

'Then we must keep Mew indoors!' Sarah said.

I nodded. 'From now on she mustn't even go out in the yard.'

Sarah pulled a slight face, turning up her nose, for she took pains to ensure that our shop and living quarters were always clean and sweet-smelling.

'She could go outside on a leash of string,' I said. 'And you or I will watch her to see that she doesn't bite through it and get away.' I held Mew at arm's length and she seemed to look at me reproachfully with her big round eyes. 'It's for your own good!' I said. 'And when all is well with the world, then you can go out properly once more.'

Tom gave a slight cough. 'Miss Hannah. I came to ask if you wished to come picking violets with me,' he said.

I smiled at him, pleased and excited to be asked.

'Where do you intend to go for them?' Sarah wanted to know.

'To Chelsea,' Tom said. 'Doctor da Silva is busy now preparing a great many remedies against the plague and he needs several herbs which only grow wild. I know you use violets a great deal yourself, and there is a patch known only to myself on the banks of the Thames there.'

I glanced at Sarah, who was nodding. 'Violets – yes, we always need many!' she said. 'It has been harder to buy them at the market lately. And if you should see any wild strawberries, Hannah, or borage, I would have some of those too.' She glanced at Tom. 'But of course Master Tom must have first pick.'

Tom smiled. 'There is plenty enough to go round,' he said. 'I know all the secret places.' He patted the canvas bag which he carried over his shoulder. 'This will be full by the time we come home.'

Sarah found me a trug, and asked me in a low voice if I would rather not change out of my green gown and into another more modest one. I stopped her words with a frown and shake of my head, however, and she smiled and let me go.

Chelsea was about five miles away but a pleasant walk once we got through the press of London, and it only took us just over an hour to reach the meadows

Tom had spoken of. We talked all the way. Tom told me about Doctor da Silva, saying that he was a clever man and a good master to his apprentices – which seemed just as well, for Tom still had another four of his seven years to serve. He told me that his mother had died in childbirth several years ago, his father had married again and it was then that Tom had been bound to the doctor.

''Twas to get me away from home, for my stepmother can't abide me,' he said. 'She has no time for the children born to my father before she came.'

I hadn't had such an interesting life, but I told Tom about my family in Chertsey, and how Sarah and I were faring in the shop, and also about meeting Abby again. Then I told him about our visit to the Exchange and all the elegant and fashionable people we'd seen.

'There won't be so many of these elegant people around soon,' Tom said. 'Now that the king and his court have left London, they'll all be going after them.'

This led to us talking about the plague, and I asked what remedies were most effective. Tom said that everyone had different ideas. 'Some say the best thing is to hold a coin of gold in your mouth whenever you go out – and the best of these is an angel from Elizabeth's reign,' he said.

I shook my head, astonished. 'I have never even seen a gold angel,' I said, 'much less have a spare one to put in my mouth!'

'There are many other remedies. You can hold a piece of nutmeg in your mouth. Or a sprig of rosemary. Or a clove,' he said, laughing. 'Or a roasted fig, or some tobacco, or a quantity of snails without their shells.'

I shuddered.

'The doctor has all cures for all prices. For the rich he will provide a cordial made from unicorn's horns and honey, for the poor a decoction of clover and cat's-foot. There is a great deal of money to be made from the plague.'

'So is he a quack, then – your doctor?' I asked wonderingly.

Tom shook his head. 'Of course not. What he prescribes he truly believes in.'

'What then will *you* take against the plague?'

He thought for some time. 'The seeds and leaves of cornflowers taken in wine are said to be most effective for those born under my planet.'

'And should I take the same?'

'You're a sun subject – so the doctor told me,' he said, and I felt a moment's pleasure at the knowledge that he had been talking about me. He thought for a moment, frowning. It caused a small line to appear between his eyes which I had a longing to smooth out with my finger. 'The peony is a flower of the sun,' he said at last, 'though I have not studied enough to know . . .' His face cleared, 'but it is well known that chopped with rue it will promote pleasant dreams and take away fears, and this is all to the good.'

I nodded. 'And where shall I get these things?'

'I shall steep the leaves and begin making you a decoction tomorrow, Hannah.'

There it was again, his voice, saying my name in that soft way. I stopped walking, turned to him, and caught him staring at me. We smiled at each other and I felt a shiver run through me, moving down my spine like a trickle of iced water. He said nothing, but he caught hold of my hand and held it to his face for a moment before letting it go. I felt that we both wanted to say or do something but, ignorant of what this thing should be, we just walked on.

Chelsea was a pretty little village on the Thames, its thatched cottages, farms and uncrowded streets reminding me a little of Chertsey. A field fronted the river, a field thick with lush grass and bright with starry white daisies and golden marigolds. Tom led me through this pasture to the river edge where green rushes grew thickly, and tangled masses of reeds floated out like green hair. We took off our shoes and sat peaceably for some time with our feet in the water, watching the river craft go by and listening to the birdsong. I said there seemed to be more boats about and Tom told me that because of the fear of plague, many people had taken to the river, intending to live on barges and makeshift craft until the danger was over.

Tom had a list of flowers and herbs which the doctor needed. These included angelica, cornflowers, wild garlic, scabious, chervil and sage, all of which he said would be used in plague remedies. Along the edges of the field and in certain places already known to Tom he collected these, snipping off the flower heads and putting them into muslin bags and then into his canvas holdall. Afterwards, he showed me where the patches of wild violets were, and helped me gather a large number to put in my trug. There were many borage flowers, too, which I knew Sarah wanted to candy. Tom took some of these as well, for he said that an infusion made from the flowers expelled melancholy. 'The doctor always says that a merry heart does good like a medicine,' he added.

Setting off for home, we were light-hearted, but as we neared London an invisible pall seemed to gather over us and stifle our laughter. A stillness lay upon the city (Sunday being the day of atonement) as if it was waiting, hushed, for something to befall it. I shivered for I knew now that this thing was plague.

As we reached the shop Tom moved near to me, took a lock of my hair and, looking into my eyes, curled a ringlet around his finger so that I had to move my face closer and closer to his. I was quite breathless, thinking he was about to kiss me, when suddenly there came down the quiet street the loud clattering of clogs on cobbles, and Tom and I sprang apart from each other. Two women appeared – but such women! Frightening old hags, clad in sacking, with deep hoods over their heads, carrying long white staves in front of them.

I instinctively shrank back, fearing their very appearance, and Tom did too, pressing into the shop doorway beside me.

'Who are they?' I asked with a shiver as they passed us. 'Where are they going?'

'They are the searchers of the dead,' Tom said. I looked at him, alarmed, and he added, 'They are employed by the parish. In the event of a death it is their gruesome duty to search the body and ascertain why that person has died. If they find the plague marks on them then the sexton has a grave prepared and sees that their house is shut up for forty days.'

'But there have been no cases of plague round here!'

His expression grew solemn. 'I fear there may have been,' he said. He squeezed my hand. 'But go in and tell your sister what you've seen – she may know something further.' He caught my eyes and smiled. 'Try to be of good heart whatever the news is. I shall call on you with your cordial as soon as it is made.'

Chapter Six

The second week of July

'But Lord, how everybody's looks and discourse in the street is of Death and nothing else.'

When I went inside there was just one taper burning in our back room, and Sarah was sitting quietly on our bed, her hands folded in her lap.

'What is it?' I asked, alarmed, for normally she would have been busy doing something: weighing up sugar, writing the accounts or mending an apron. Now, though, she was just sitting there, her face shocked and pale.

I put down the trug and went towards her. 'I saw two horrible old women on the road. Tom told me they were searchers of the dead. Did you see them? Where have they been?'

Sarah's hands clenched into fists. 'They've been nearby, Hannah. In the first alley off Crown and King Place.'

'And where did they search?'

She looked down. 'In the old house hard by the sign

of the Blue Goose.'

'Dickon and Jacob's house?'

She nodded. 'It was the babe. Their little sister Marie—'

I gasped. 'Not—'

Sarah swallowed hard. 'She was taken poorly only yesterday, but her mother, Mrs Williams, told no one for fear they'd call in the authorities. She said it looked like just a rash. She thought it was a sweating sickness. But then this morning two buboes came up on the child's body.'

'What are they?' I asked fearfully.

'Hard lumps of matter. They come up in the groin, or in the neck or under the arm.' She hesitated. 'They are a sure sign of plague.'

'And then what happened?'

'Mrs Williams called for an apothecary, for they couldn't afford a doctor. And it wasn't Doctor da Silva, it was someone else. But before he could arrive the buboes had become so engorged with matter that the baby could not move its legs or head without screaming.'

I shuddered.

'And although the apothecary tried to lance the buboes it was too late. They said she screamed out one last time – the most terrible sound – and then died.'

I pulled up a stool and sat next to Sarah, not saying anything for some moments, trying to absorb and understand what this meant. I hardly knew Marie, for she was barely two years old and had not been walking long enough to be out and about much with Dickon and Jacob. I'd just seen a sturdy, grubby, child staggering about the place trying to catch hold of one of the cats. Once I'd given her a few candied rose petals and she'd gabbled in baby-talk at me and run off.

After a while I asked Sarah to tell me more of the tale.

'The first I knew that the child had ... that is, the first I knew what had happened was that the bells of St Dominic's started tolling. And then Mr Newbery banged on the door here and shouted that there had been a terrible event. I went outside and everyone seemed to be at their doors, just standing there, silently. I went from house to house asking what had happened, but they were all crying and could hardly tell me. And then Mrs Williams ran into the street. She was tearing at her clothes and screaming, pulling her hair out like she was going mad with grief. Only then did someone tell me it was Marie who had died, and it was thought to be of the plague.'

I went to our fireplace and put the kettle on to boil so I could make some camomile tea for us both. I felt cold and hollow, hardly believing what had happened. How could that child be among us one moment, running about happily, and dead the next?

'The worst thing,' Sarah went on, 'is that this poor woman ... this mother quite demented by grief...could mayhap have been comforted by someone's voice soothing her and telling her that she must look now to her other children, but no one would go near her.'

'She has no husband,' I said, remembering what Sarah had told me about Jacob's father being a sailor, and dying at sea earlier in the year.

Sarah shook her head. 'No husband, no comforter at all. I felt I wanted to do something for her, put my arms around her and console her, but I could not bring myself. The fear of the plague was too great. And so she suffers in her grief alone.' Sarah began crying. 'But you have not heard the worst,' she added – and I knew it was selfish of me but I immediately looked round to see where Mew was.

'It's not Mew,' she said, shaking her head through her tears. 'He's in a box under our bed and hasn't been out.'

'What, then? Tell me quickly,' I begged her.

'The eldest child has it. Kate – she has the same symptoms. And their house is being shut up.'

'Oh,' I breathed.

We were both silent as we waited for the water to boil. I tried to imagine how it would be in that house, with Mrs Williams just sitting and waiting for the signs of plague to appear, waiting to see if Death would visit any other of her children.

'What if *she* dies?' I asked suddenly. 'What if Mrs Williams dies next and the children have to fend for themselves alone, shut up in the house?'

Sarah shook her head. 'I don't know. Maybe they will all be taken to the pesthouse – although there are not many of those and I hear they are already full.'

'Is their house already closed?'

'I fear so,' Sarah said. 'And now they must stay inside for forty days.'

'The boys will hate that.'

Sarah glanced up at me and I knew what she was thinking: they would probably be visited with plague and die before then.

'Maybe we could give them something,' I said suddenly.

She nodded. 'I was thinking that. Something to cheer the children, perhaps. Some comfits.'

The kettle was rattling on the fire, so I poured boiling water on the camomile flowers and let it steep for a few moments. 'Even if the house is already locked and barred, we could ask their guard to give them the sweetmeats.'

Sarah dabbed at her eyes with her apron and stood up. 'It will make us feel better if we do something – even just some little thing – for the family,' she said. 'What flowers did you harvest today?'

I showed her the trug and its contents, and while we drank our tea I told her something of my hours with Tom, and how thoughtful and pleasant a companion he was. I did not tell her of the times when we'd been rapt in each other's glances, however, for they were private moments, for me to think on later.

I changed into my working dress and Sarah busied herself putting more water on to boil in a pan, then she chipped a goodly piece of sugar from a new loaf and put that in as well. 'Tomorrow we will begin to candy some borage flowers,' she said, 'for they are said to have virtues which may help lighten their hearts. Tonight, though, we'll make some little violet cakes. And we will take them to the house together and try not to be alarmed at anything we might see.' She shook the pan to help dissolve the sugar. 'Whatever fright we take will be nothing compared to what they are going through.'

She set me to nipping the violet flowers from their stalks and washing them, while she boiled the water to melt the sugar. Several times she skimmed it of foam, until it was a thick, clear syrup mixture. Then I was allowed to take the violets – about a quarter of all I'd picked – stir them thoroughly in the mixture, then quickly pour it out into a wetted tray.

The mixture began to harden almost immediately and we let it be while we washed the rest of the violets and borage flowers for the next day. When we turned to it again the flat cake was almost firm, and Sarah carefully cut it into small squares, lifted them from the tray and put them on white paper. They looked very pretty, for I had made sure to choose a variety of colours for the violets, and they ranged from white through pink down to deepest purple. Not, I realised, that it was likely that our poor family would appreciate this careful harmonising of colour.

When the violet cakes were quite cool we folded them into a small package and set off for the house. The windows and door were already barred, and marked with the red cross. Above the cross I could see the same paper sign that I'd seen on the house in St Giles: LORD, HAVE MERCY ON US.

Sarah and I held each other's hands tightly as we approached, for I can't convey how much fear was struck into us to see these words so close to home, and to imagine the terror of that little family on the other side of the door.

The guard, a youngish bearded man, was sitting outside on a stool, his halberd standing diagonally across the doorway of the house.

'Could you give these sweetmeats to the children next time you see them?' Sarah asked, giving the package into his hands.

He nodded. 'That will be in the morning,' he said, 'when I takes in their milk and bread.'

'Are they . . .' I hesitated. I'd been about to ask if they were all right, but of course they were not, and I did not know what else to say.

'They're sleeping now,' he said. 'An apothecary has given them all a draught.'

I was torn between wanting to make our stay there as brief as possible and finding out more, but Sarah was already pulling at my hand to come away.

We walked to our shop, looking back only once at the enclosed and silent house.

'Violet cakes – they seem but poor reparation,' Sarah said. 'What can they do to help?'

I shrugged. 'I don't know.'

But we were glad we had gone.

The following day we took some candied borage flowers up to the house and left them with the guard, but had no way of knowing whether they actually received them or whether the guard ate them himself.

The Bills for that week showed 750 deaths in London and to our great dismay our trade began falling off a little. This was because many of our customers, being mostly of the middling classes, knew how to obtain a Certificate of Health, and were going to their country houses. The king and his court moved further out, too – from Isleworth to Hampton Court – for it had been said that Isleworth was not far enough away from the contamination in London and it was feared the plague might still be able to reach him there.

On Saturday a fruit-seller came to our door calling,

'Cherry-ripe!' and although Sarah said they were too early to be Kentish cherries, and must have come on a ship from the Netherlands, she bought some on my urging, for I was anxious to try out the recipe for sugared cherries which mother had given me. After washing a scoopful of these, I carefully stoned and halved them, then set them over the heat in a preserving pan with a little water. When they were scalding hot I shook them in a sieve, then put them in a cloth to dry, after which I put them back into the pan, layered with a good amount of sugar that I had previously ground down. Putting this pan back on the fire, I scalded the cherries and cooled them three times all together, so that they picked up the sugar and it crystallised on them. After this I dipped them quickly in cold water and placed them in the hot sun to dry out.

Sarah watched me and said this was a new recipe for her, and she had not worked with cherries before, but thought they looked very pretty and tasty.

That evening came the information from Mr Newbery that there had been another death at the top of our street, although as the person there had lived alone there was no need for the house to be shut up. We had received no further news of our Williams family these last three days, so as we closed the shutter of the shop, Sarah and I resolved that we would go and enquire after them.

The guard outside their house was asleep and snoring, so Sarah tapped on the next-door house to enquire how they did.

The woman who answered, Mrs Groat, shook her head. 'I've heard nothing of them these last two days,' she said. 'That first night – and the next day – there was a wailing and a crying and carrying on, but for the last two days there's been nothing.'

'Has food been taken inside?' Sarah asked.

She shrugged. 'The guard has money to buy their everyday provisions, and get milk for the children, but to tell the truth I fear he takes it for ale. I was going to ask the minister at church tomorrow what I should do.' She looked at us and lowered her voice, 'I don't even know if they live.'

Hearing this, Sarah did no more than go straight to the guard outside the Williams' house and try to rouse him, and I fear he *had* been on ale, for it took a great deal of shaking and shouting before he was awake to our questions.

'We want to know how the family within are,' she said and, seeing his rather blank and stupid face, added some falsely polite words of praise for his care of them.

'Has a doctor called on them?' I asked, thinking that if nothing else I could run and get Doctor da Silva and see what he could do.

The man smiled, a drunken, lop-sided smile. 'This family give me no trouble at all. Quiet as the flowers, they are.'

'But we want to know if they're all right!' Sarah said. 'When did you last see them?'

'Can you ask them how they're doing?' I said. 'Can we see if they need anything?'

The man leaned over and picked up his glittering halberd, waving it in front of our faces. 'I has to guard this house. No one can go in!'

'*You* can go in, though, can't you?' I said. 'You can

see how they fare.'

He looked at us suspiciously. 'Are you family?'

I was about to say no, but Sarah broke in and said yes, they were our dear cousins and we were fair desperate to know how they were doing.

'We hoped such a kind and reasonable man as yourself would be looking after them,' I added, for I could see that flattery might be the only thing to move him. 'Would you be able give us news on how they fare?'

Grinning now, the man got out a set of keys and proceeded to open the two padlocks which held together the chains which had been hammered across the doorway. He pushed at the door, which opened to nothing but silence and darkness.

'How do you keep?' the guard hollered into the hallway. 'Is there owt you need?'

Holding each other, Sarah and I looked through into the hall, where not a candle or a taper showed through the darkness. And then the air from the newly-opened house billowed to reach us and we smelled a stench so foetid that we had to step backwards.

'I very much fear all is not well,' she whispered to me, and then braced herself to call, 'Hello! Mrs Williams. Is there anything you need?'

No reply came.

She and I looked at each other nervously, for I felt sick from the smell and would not have been brave enough to enter.

'Will you go in?' Sarah asked the guard.

'Not I!' he said. 'I'm not paid to enter charnel houses.'

'And you mustn't go in either!' I said, holding fast to Sarah's arm.

Behind us, Mrs Groat had come up to peer into the dark abyss of the house.

'I'd best shut 'm up again,' the guard said, but there was suddenly a tremendous crash from inside the house, making us all cry out in fear, and the next moment a small pale figure jumped or fell down the stairs and shot past us, running down the cobbled streets as if the devil himself was after him.

'A ghoul!' Mrs Groat said, and she fell to her knees and began praying.

'No!' I said, looking after the boy in disbelief. 'It was little Dickon!'

'Stark naked and running for his life,' Sarah said.

I watched his progress down the street and would have turned to go after him, but Sarah knew what was in my mind and held me fast. 'You must not,' she said. 'He will have the plague on his skin.'

'But who will look after him?'

'It can't be us! If you catch him it will be a death warrant for us both.'

When we turned back the guard was standing in the doorway, still reluctant to enter. He sniffed and then curled his nostrils in disgust. 'I smell death!' he said.

'You must go and see,' Sarah insisted. 'We cannot just shut the house now. You must go and see who's dead.'

After some persuasion – and Sarah had some small coins on her which we handed to him – he went inside and came back a few moments later to tell us that there were two children dead in a bed upstairs, and the mother was lying dead by the kitchen table.

As the news spread, a small crowd gathered outside the house, most of whom were openly crying. Sarah, brushing back tears herself, asked one of them to go down to the minister so that women could be called in to dress the bodies and make them ready for burial.

We went home, but could not sleep for thinking about the poor, dead children and for wondering what had become of young Dickon. We were not to find this out, however, for we never saw nor heard a word of him again.

Chapter Seven

The third week of July

'But how sad a sight it is to see the streets empty of people, and very few upon the 'Change . . . and two shops in three shut up.'

When we closed shop on the day following the Williams family's deaths, Sarah and I resolved to go along to their house to try and discover when their funeral would be, for she said it was not right that a mother and her innocent children should be buried with no one to cast flowers into their graves.

We had enquired after Dickon that day, but had failed to find any trace of him, and Sarah had said that we must try to think that a kindly family somewhere were looking after him, or at least that he'd been taken to a workhouse or pesthouse for shelter. Neither of us wanted to think that he might still be on the streets of London, frightened, naked and hungry; that he might have ended up living in the sewers with the rats, or on the edge of the stinking Fleet ditch at Westminster where, Sarah said, the river ran thick and stagnant and the poorest, foulest beggars ended up, living on peelings and scraps.

At the Williams' house the wooden boarding had gone from the door and windows, and the fearful red cross had been replaced by a white one to signify modified quarantine, although it would be twenty days and the house would have to be fumigated before anyone could live in it. There was no man guarding it now, but neither were there any housewives chattering outside or children playing nearby. It seemed that people passing knew of the deaths, for they were walking in an arc past the house, as far away as they could get, as if they were trying to avoid breathing any of the air coming from it.

When we asked at the adjoining dwelling, Mrs Groat came to her door with a full pipe of tobacco in her hand which she puffed continually as she spoke. She apologised for doing so. 'But I have heard that it is the only true prevention against the plague,' she said, 'and I am not going to be seen without it all the while people are dropping faster than flies.'

'We came to enquire about the children's funeral,' Sarah said, standing back so as not to be enveloped in smoke.

Mrs Groat shook her head. 'There will be no funeral,' she said, 'for the mayor has issued orders that there must be no gatherings of people.'

'But there must be some small ceremony!' Sarah said, concerned. 'At least a minister must stand by their grave and offer up a prayer to send them on their way.'

'I think not,' the old woman said. She coughed a little herself with the smoke. 'There have been so many funerals already that now they are saying the dead must be dispatched with as little ceremony as possible. All that will mark their passing will be the tolling of a bell.'

'But there haven't been that many deaths in this parish, surely?' I asked.

Mrs Groat shrugged. 'Two in Crutched Friars Alley yesterday. *Said* to be dead of the fever,' she added meaningfully. 'Then our poor Williams family, a house at the sign of the Crooked Bear – there are four dead there, two dead in the Shambles, and one dead in a house just newly shut up in Stinking Lane. They say that at St Dominic's there's been funerals every day for two weeks.'

'I had no idea,' Sarah said in a shocked voice, while I tried to take in these numbers. As if to confirm what she was saying, I could hear, from several points across the city, the dull tolling of church bells.

The woman lowered her voice. 'It's said that St Dominic's and the smaller churchyards will soon be filled to overflowing, so they won't be able to take more bodies. And what will happen then? My husband says they'll just be left in the houses to rot!'

Sarah and I gasped.

'They're already collecting the bodies in a cart instead of on a pallet,' she went on. 'They came last night for the children and took them all of a heap together.'

Sarah and I looked at each other. 'Then it's far, far worse than we thought,' she said to me in a voice a little above a whisper.

Mrs Groat nodded. 'Aye,' she said. 'I fear we've all been deceiving ourselves. My husband and I would go out of town if we could – but where would we go? Who is going to take in someone from this city when God knows what airs and humours we're carrying on us? Besides, we could not afford the certificates.'

Sarah asked which brand of tobacco Mrs Groat was using and she told us, though I could not imagine me or Sarah smoking a stinking pipe, or even how you managed to smoke and breathe at the same time without choking to death.

We wished the woman well (though privately wondered if the poor thing had already contracted the plague by being so close to the contagion) and began to walk back to the shop. We had work to do, for we had almost used up our supply of rose water and must make a quantity soon, for it was needed in almost every recipe we used for our sweetmeats.

We passed a sedan chair carrying someone being taken to a pesthouse, with a man in front holding a white stave and clanging a bell to warn people to keep out of the way. As we stood back to watch it pass Sarah linked her arm with mine and drew me close. 'I feel so guilty about bringing you here and making you go through all this, Hannah,' she said. 'If only you'd received my second letter before you left Chertsey.'

'But if I wasn't here you'd be all on your own!' I protested. 'It wouldn't be right if you had no one to befriend you. Besides,' I hesitated a moment, then said, 'if you fell ill, who would look after you?'

What I didn't say – for I was ashamed of even having such a feeling – was that I *wanted* to be here, that I found it dangerous and exciting to be in London at this hour. Some of this was to do with having met Tom, and some to do with the heightened sense of tension and anxiety that now seemed to surround us. At home in Chertsey, life had been peaceful. The milk turning sour or getting blackfly on our beans had been the only disturbances to our calm existence. Here, though, *now*, there was a bitter, heart-stopping danger in each day. We were walking on the very edge of a chasm of fire.

We had been to market that morning but had not gone very early, as we usually did in order to get the freshest blooms, for Sarah had said that to make rose water it hardly mattered what condition the flowers were in. We had gone, then, to find bargains rather than perfection. The blooms we'd bought had been placed in enamel jugs of water outside our back door and when I went to get them in (first checking on Mew, who was safely under the bed) Sarah suggested that before we started making rose water, we should take some of our blooms down to St Dominic's churchyard.

'No matter if the family are not having a proper funeral,' she said. 'We can at least say a prayer over the graves of those children.'

We took one red rose for Mrs Williams, and three pink roses: one for Kate, one for Jacob and one for Marie, and walked along to the churchyard with them. It was a warm night and not yet dark – the watchman called eight of the clock as we walked – but there was hardly anyone about.

'They are staying indoors,' Sarah said. 'And have you seen how people now try to avoid each other in the street?'

I nodded, for I'd already noticed that during this last week or two, people would step in the kennel ditch muck in the middle of the roadway rather than come face to face, breath to breath, with someone who might be infected with the sickness.

We talked of our family in Chertsey as we walked, and both fervently hoped and prayed that the plague would not reach them there.

'And even if I got a Certificate of Health, how could I go back home now?' I asked Sarah. 'I could be carrying the plague on my clothes.' I looked down at myself. 'I could be carrying it from London into our home and give it to our brothers and sisters.'

Sarah shook her head slowly. 'No, I can see we are both here for the duration, so we must follow all the rules. We must keep the space in front of our shop swept clean, and take care not to eat anything unwholesome. We must examine our bodies carefully each night to make sure no spots or lumps appear. We will chew a sprig of rosemary when we go abroad, and we will take a cordial and make ourselves an ABRACADABRA talisman, for I hear they are most effective.'

I nodded. 'One other thing – when I went to the grocer's I found I had to put my payment coins into a jar of vinegar.'

Sarah nodded. 'Then we shall have our customers do that, too,' she said. 'With care, you and I can survive.'

I smiled back at her and squeezed her hand. I was full of optimism and could not believe I could die, for I had everything to live for.

The bell was tolling mournfully as we approached our parish church, and over the small lychgate which led into the graveyard a tall wax candle burned.

Hearing noises and looking over the wall, we discovered four men digging a large hole. To one side there was a piece of tarpaulin on which – my heart contracted – seven corpses were lain. These were not enclosed in wooden coffins, but wound in rough shrouds with a clumsy knot tied at each end.

I clutched Sarah's hand, and nodded towards them, my teeth beginning to chatter with fright. I had seen dead corpses before, but only one at a time, and then each body had been settled, washed and neat, arms crossed at the breast, in a pine coffin. These corpses, though, were just piled carelessly on one side like stale loaves.

'Oh, we should not have come!' Sarah said in a low and shaky voice. 'We should have stayed away from this horror.'

'Do you think that is . . . is *them*?' I asked, nodding towards the corpses.

'Maybe,' she whispered. 'Them and some others.'

'Or maybe our family were buried yesterday,' I said, looking across the churchyard. 'Look at all the new mounds!'

There were many piles of freshly-dug earth, but no way of telling if each held more than one body. Some sort of white powder had been strewn across the whole churchyard, and it covered the ground like snow.

'It's lime,' Sarah said in answer to my question. 'Lime to stop the infection and to encourage the bodies to . . . to . . .' she shuddered and could not finish.

The men were still digging steadily, throwing the earth to one side and singing a bawdy song as they worked. They did not acknowledge us in any way.

'Shall we . . . shall we ask if the bodies they are burying are those of the Williams family?' I asked.

Sarah shook her head. 'They will have no way of knowing who they bury. And as there seems to be no clergy to ask, I think we may as well go home. We can do no good here, and it fair turns my stomach to see such things.'

'Let us throw in our flowers before we go, then,' I said.

Sarah nodded. 'And say our own prayer.'

So we leaned over the wall and threw in our roses, and the grave-diggers, on seeing us, fell silent. I said a prayer for the Williams family, and then we went home.

When the Bills were published, we found out that one thousand people had died from plague during that week.

'One thousand!' everyone whispered in shocked voices, although it had quickly become common knowledge that this figure was much lower than it should have been. Mr Newbery told us that the bereaved would bribe the searchers of the dead to have a death recorded as spotted fever or the purples, rather than have plague noted against the name and cause the rest of the family to be shut up for forty days. Most of the searchers, he told us, were brutal and common types who would sell their own mothers for a flagon of gin.

That day was a black one for us, too, for Mew disappeared. I had hardly been in our back room at all as I had spent the morning in the shop making orange-flower water: boiling water on our fire, steeping the orange blossom in it, then straining and re-straining the resulting pale primrose liquid through muslin. At dinner time Sarah bought a pigeon pie from a pie-man, and when we went into the back, calling for Mew to come and have a scrap with us, she wasn't there on the end of her tethering string. Discovering this, Sarah and I stared at each other in horror.

'Was she there this morning?' she asked me.

I nodded. 'I gave her some bread and milk. Her string was tied tightly – I checked it!' I assured her.

We looked under the bed and, finding that Mew had wriggled her head through the neck loop, both began to cry.

'One of the catchers has taken her – I know they have!' I said. I was already imagining her sad fate, for I had seen a creaking old farm cart the day before stacked to the brim with the carcasses of dogs and cats in a carelessly jumbled pile of fur and hair.

We looked around the room carefully, in case she was hiding herself (although there were precious few secret places). Then Sarah looked out the front door while I went to the back. I searched our yard and privy, and called, 'Mew!' across the roofs several times, all the while banging one of our old bowls with a spoon to try and attract her. Our yard stayed empty, though, and I thought sadly that if we'd have done the same thing just two weeks ago, a stable-load of cats and kits would have come to our door to be fed.

Sitting down, we ate some of our pigeon pie, although found we had little appetite for it.

Sarah sighed. 'We must imagine to ourselves that,

like Dickon, Mew has gone to a happier home,' she said. 'Maybe she's jumped on a cart and gone out of town, or maybe she's got herself into a cosy household where meat is on the menu every day.'

I nodded, my heart heavy. What I was thinking and was scared to say was, what would happen if, after a day or so, Mew came back? We wouldn't know where she'd been. She might have been scratching for mice in a newly-dug churchyard beside a body rotten with plague, or have lodged a while in a house struck down with it. Maybe her thick grey fur would be harbouring the very sickness that we dreaded so much.

But Mew did not come back, and it seemed certain that she'd slipped her string to go after a mouse or two and been found by one of the fat-gutted ruffians who were employed on the shameful job of clubbing animals to death. Sarah and I cried ourselves to sleep that night, but after that we did not speak of her again, for it seemed to be tempting fate to mourn the loss of a kitten when all around us people were losing parents, children, brothers and sisters.

More and more people were departing for the country. One morning I had an errand to run for Sarah which took me along the Tyburn Road, and I saw several coach-and-fours laden with cases and servants, trundling along with their thick brocade curtains closed tight to protect the occupants from the stares of the common people. I knew that the travellers must all be either of the aristocracy, or at least affluent merchants or rich landowners, for apart from the fact of their having a coach and horses of their own, and a place to go in the country, I had not heard of an ordinary person being able to obtain a health certificate.

I saw, too, a pretty yellow-varnished carriage sway past me pulled by two chestnut horses, their manes and tails tied with green ribbon, and the coachman wearing smart green livery. I glanced inside, for this time the curtains were not closed, and was sure I saw Nelly Gwyn sitting there in a peacock-blue gown, for the girl looked up just at that moment and though her ribboned bonnet partly obscured her face, I could see a flash of unruly red hair.

Sarah laughed when I told her this and said I had just seen what I wanted to see, but I am sure it *was* Nelly, for her carriage was heading towards Salisbury, and we had heard that the king and his court were on their way there to be further off still from London. I like to think she was obeying an invitation from His Majesty to come and dance some lively jigs for the gentlemen of the court to console them for being away from the entertainments in the capital.

That day, walking back from my errand which was to obtain an amount of rose oil from a grocer, I could not help my ears being assailed by the constant tolling of the church bells announcing more deaths, or seeing the red crosses on doors as I passed. Most of these doors were in the poorer parts of the city – although not all, for I saw a substantial house in Blackfriars which had been enclosed, and one big dwelling in Fleet Street also. In this house someone had dislodged a plank over the first-floor window and from this space two small, tear-stained children peered out, scared and bewildered. I could not help but wonder what was happening within. Had their mother and father succumbed to the disease? Who was looking after them? There was no way of telling and no one seemed to care.

Two more things I noticed. One was the activity in the churchyards, for each contained at least two grave-diggers going about their gruesome business, and some had been dug over so constantly for new burials that they resembled ploughed fields. The other thing which assaulted the eye was the number of posters offering preventatives against the sickness. On almost every tree and shutter they hung, advertising amulets, powders, cordials, charms, pills and enchantments. There were some herbal preventatives that Tom had already told me of, and others made from all manner of strange things: powders made from dried toads, an amount of mercury contained in a walnut shell, or a talisman made from a verse from the Bible written in a certain mystical way. All promised to shield against contagion and prevent malignant humours from affecting the body.

Which of these would be effective, though?

With so much at stake, which to choose?

Seeing all these promises and writings together made me think of Tom, for I had not heard a word from him since our day out. I vowed, therefore, that I would go to Doctor da Silva's as soon as I could to ask Tom about the cordial he had said he would prepare for me. This was a good enough reason and could be my excuse, but the truth was that in spite of all that was going on around us, he filled my thoughts and I longed to see him again.

Chapter Eight

The fourth week of July

'And they tell me that in Westminster there is never a Physician and but one Apothecary, all others being dead.'

Out of the darkness of Doctor da Silva's shop a monstrous figure came towards me, causing me to scream aloud. The creature was broad and imposing, its head was that of a great bird of prey, with a tiny shining eye and a great hooked beak, and its breathing as it lumbered towards me was hoarse and rasping.

'Keep away!' I screamed. I backed away, trembling, feeling behind me for the door through which I'd just entered. I tried to recall some holy words to banish such an evil and unearthly creature, but in my panic could not think of any.

There was the sound of running feet across the shop and Tom's voice called, 'It's all right, Hannah!' he said. 'It's just Doctor da Silva.'

I burst into tears of fright and relief and Tom put his arms around me. 'It's the doctor in the outfit he uses to visit the stricken.'

I drew in a shuddering breath, peering through my fingers at the figure. Now that I could see more clearly in the dim light I discerned that it was, indeed, only a man in a strange headdress and covering gown of heavy waxed material, and not a creature from hell at all. 'Is it truly him?' I asked, for I felt comforted in Tom's arms and did not want to stir myself from them.

'Doctor, will you take off your head?' Tom asked, and the frightening creature lifted his arms and pulled off the leathery headdress of his outfit, beak and all, revealing himself indeed as the doctor.

'Yes, it is I,' he said, trying to flatten his tangled grey hair. 'I am dressed to go and treat plague victims.'

My fright disappearing, I thought I had better let my arms fall from Tom's shoulders, for I did not wish to appear too forward. 'And is this what you have to wear?' I asked breathlessly.

The doctor nodded. 'All the apothecaries and the doctors – that is, those who are still in London and have not gone away to the country with their wealthy patrons – have them now.'

'The thick gown prevents any infection touching the doctor's skin, and the beak contains strong herbs,' Tom said. 'Every breath he takes will come through these herbs and be cleansed.'

'And the herbs are . . .?' Doctor da Silva asked of Tom.

'Alehoof, ivy, sage, chervil and scabious, sire,' he answered, and the doctor nodded. He looked at me. 'And how are you and your sister, and how do you find yourself in your shop? Do you have good health?'

'We are doing quite well, I thank you,' I said.

'Though we have . . .' My voice choked in my throat and I had to pause a moment. 'We have lost some of our neighbours to the sickness.'

The doctor shook his head reflectively. 'It is said that Thursday's Bills will contain some 2,000 deaths.'

I gasped. 'But that is double that of last week!'

'And it will increase, I fear, unless they stop shutting up the houses and entombing the living with the dead,' he said.

'Doctor da Silva thinks it would be better to take the sick person off to a pesthouse and isolate him there,' Tom explained.

'Although the city is not supplied with nearly enough of those,' the doctor said grimly. 'In the meantime when one person sickens and they are shut in with their family and servants, then they *all* fall sick. There is nothing more certain. One might just as well bury them alive.'

'But can people catch the plague and live?' I asked, for this was something Sarah and I had been pondering.

'It is possible – with the right treatment at the right time. The buboes have to burst, however.' The doctor turned to Tom as he said this, looking at him enquiringly.

'A root of the Madonna lily mixed with hog's grease makes a poultice to ripen plague sores,' Tom said, on his cue.

The doctor inclined his head. 'They must burst and discharge their poison, for if they do not then the matter goes inward and infects every organ of the body.' He paused. 'What preventatives are you taking?' he asked me.

I felt my cheeks flushing. 'I came today because Tom said he would prepare me a cordial,' I said. 'I wondered if he had finished it yet.'

'The flowers had to be steeped and the liquid boiled and strained by turn. It took over a week to make,' Tom said apologetically. 'And then we have been so busy with our new patients and with making up preventatives I have not found time to bring it to you.'

'So you have been taking nothing all this while?' the doctor asked me.

'Well, Sarah and I always chew sprigs of rosemary before we go out,' I said. 'And we each have a rabbit's foot. And a cabalistic sign.' I pulled from my bodice the piece of paper on which a travelling pedlar had written ABRACADABRA in a certain way, as a magical triangle.

The doctor looked at the paper. 'I cannot think that this will help. But, Tom, what is Hannah's cordial?'

'A compound of peony flowers and cornflower leaves steeped in wine,' Tom replied. 'A general preventative, for I thought both her and Miss Sarah would take it.'

'Then fetch the bottle now, and I will delay my visits to our troubled neighbours until you have taken both her and it back safely. But be quick.'

When Tom returned with the bottle I noticed that the cordial was thick and brown and did not look very appetising, but under the doctor's eye I was given instructions for taking it. Tom and I then walked together back to the shop, seeing on the way two fellows closing up a house at Friars Alley and fastening locks and chains across the door. I told Tom of the Williams family, and of the way Dickon had burst out of the house and gone off. Tom said he had heard before of people running mad when the sickness was on them.

'I know tales of folk who have thrown themselves out of windows or run to the river and jumped in to drown themselves,' Tom said, shaking his head, 'for there is such pain while the buboes are swelling that some fair go mad with it.'

'But the doctor said that it is possible to catch the pestilence *and* survive.'

'Aye,' he said. 'If the swellings burst and heal, there is a chance. And if the tokens have not appeared.'

'What are tokens?' I asked fearfully. 'Is that another name for the buboes?'

He shook his head. 'They are little marks under the skin.'

'Like freckles?'

He smiled at me, tapping my nose with his finger. 'Not like freckles!' he said. 'Like pink blotches. They come up on the chest or arms. And if *they* appear then there is no hope at all, even if the buboes have burst.'

Our hands touched and, saying nothing, we linked our little fingers so that no one else could see. 'But how are you faring within yourself, Hannah?' he asked me. 'Tell me truly.'

I sighed and told him about Mew, and he said that the doctor had two pet dogs which had also been taken by the catchers. 'It is sad,' he said, 'but if this helps the spread of the disease, then this is what must happen.'

On our way back I noticed several shops had been shut up, including a grocer where we sometimes got our sugar, and I wondered aloud what would happen if more and more of them closed, and where we would buy our provisions.

'It will be difficult,' Tom said, 'for already there are many less pie-sellers and hawkers around. We have heard a rumour that Leadenhall Market might close because the country farmers are no longer willing to come into the city with their goods.'

'So what will happen if we can't get food?'

Tom shrugged. 'I suppose the city authorities will feed us somehow – at least with our daily bread,' he said. 'Although the doctor says that very little provision has been made. There are no public funds for relief of the poor, and no grain stored against such an event.' There was a moment's silence, then he looked at me sympathetically. 'But were you very frightened when you saw the doctor in his outfit?'

'I was!' I made myself shiver in what I hoped was an appealing way. 'I thought he was a fiend from hell!'

Tom laughed. 'Yes, he can be. But he's a good master.'

We reached the shop and Sarah, looking out and seeing that Tom was with me, bade him come in, saying that it was nearly midday and he might like to take some dinner with us.

'Thank you – but the doctor has asked me to go straight back,' Tom said to her. 'And I have many potions and preventatives to make up.'

'Another time, then,' Sarah said. She turned and busied herself over the fire, tactfully averting her eyes from us as we parted. My mouth felt dry, for I could see a certain look in Tom's eyes and was very nervous as to whether he would try to kiss me and if I should allow it.

He told me to take all necessary precautions against the sickness and said that he would see me as soon as he was able, then leaned forward and quickly brushed across my cheek with his lips. I was cross with myself afterwards, for I offered my cheek to him so quickly that he actually ended up kissing one of the ribbons on my cap.

But then again, perhaps I should not have allowed him such freedom anyway. I resolved that I would ask Abby, and went in thinking that for the last four whole minutes I had managed to forget about the plague altogether.

Three days later – for there was much to do and, as Sarah was rather low in spirits, I did not wish to leave her – I went up with our water jugs to Bell Court, hoping to see Abby. There was water to be obtained closer, but I knew she favoured this place and I was anxious to know how she was faring.

She was not in the queue for water, however, which was half as long as it usually was, for a great many of the quality had gone out of town now, either taking their servants or leaving them to fend for themselves. I could remember where she lived, so leaving my jugs unfilled for the moment, I made my way there. As I passed the various churches: St Bride's, All Hallows, St Sepulchre's, each was tolling its bell to tell of someone's passing.

I would not have dared to knock at the front door of the house, but there was a young boy in the yard grooming one of the horses, and I asked him if Abby was at home. He ran off and a few moments later came back with Abby behind him.

To my great relief – for there had been a horrid dread in my mind – she looked perfectly fine and healthy. We hugged and I said I'd been anxious about her, having not seen her at the conduit.

She pointed to a well in the yard. 'Mr Beauchurch says we must use this water now and not gather in Bell Court. He says that being in crowds is dangerous.' She pulled a face. 'And so I have to miss my afternoon gossips!'

She took my arm and we walked across the yard into the coolness of the dairy, which was a big, airy room tiled in blue and white. Milk churns stood along the floor, and there was a butter and cheese maker, and several big round wheels of cheese. 'But Hannah, what d'you think!' she said excitedly. 'I am to travel to Dorchester with my mistress and the babe!'

'Where is Dorchester?' I asked, for I had never heard of it.

'It's in Dorsetshire, southwest of London. We are to go to a great estate belonging to my mistress's sister, who is a titled lady, and there we will be safe from the sickness.'

'Oh,' I said, feeling a little forlorn. 'When will you go?'

'As soon as the mistress is well enough to travel.'

'And just you with her?'

She nodded. 'Mrs Beauchurch says that out of all the servants, I am best with the babe.' She smiled. 'For sure having six little sisters has helped me there.'

'But what about your master – doesn't he want to travel out of London as well?'

'He has to stay at his mercers' company to run the business,' she said. 'Besides, only two travel certificates can be obtained, and they are fearfully difficult to get because they have to be signed by the Lord Mayor himself. No other signatures are being accepted!' She danced a few steps around the floor. 'Just think, it will take four days to travel there and we have to stay at inns along the road, where I shall meet all sorts of young gallants!'

I laughed at her, for she was twirling around and lifting her petticoats as if she was ribbon-dancing around the maypole at home. 'But what about your sweetheart?'

She pulled a face. 'He's nothing but a niggardly hog-grubber,' she said. 'I've seen him walking out with one of the girls from the coffee shop.'

I was quiet for a moment. 'I shall miss you,' I said. 'But when do you think your mistress will be well enough to travel?'

'Next week, maybe. Though she was monstrous sick in the night and I had to go into her three times.'

'But is the babe well?'

'Aye. Healthy and hungry.'

Just then, a very well-rounded woman in a maroon gown, and a young girl in a black servant's dress, came through the dairy, both carrying shopping baskets. The fat woman frowned slightly at Abby, who just gave a beaming smile in return.

'All the house are very jealous that I'm going to Dorchester!' Abby whispered, and then laughed aloud. 'Lord, but did you see the size of Cook? That gown sits on her as tight as the skin on a plum.' She slipped towards the back doorway of the dairy. 'Come on – almost everyone's out now, and the mistress is asleep. Come in and I'll show you all the furnishings!'

* * *

The house was very large, the largest and grandest I'd ever been in. Beyond the dairy was a still room, with bunches of herbs drying and blossoms being prepared for pot-pourri and flower water, and beyond that a laundry, with ropes on which aired white linen smocks and damask bed-sheets. There was a kitchen and dining room on the next floor, but we did not go into these because Abby said the housekeeper was around. We tiptoed up to the next floor and Abby opened the door to the drawing room, showing walls hung with black and silver striped silk, delicate carved furniture and small settles bearing purple velvet cushions shot with silver. There were many portraits, too, although Abby said she didn't know who they were, and thick patterned rugs covered the floor.

The next room was even more sumptuous, with diamond-paned windows which overlooked the flowered courtyard below and a vast carved wood fireplace which reached the ceiling. This room had silver-gilt chairs and nests of drawers patterned in flowers, with Chinese vases and silver candlesticks atop, and was all very fine, so that I could not but gasp at the beauty of it all. 'I never thought furnishings of a house could be so elegant,' I said to Abby, for indeed all the houses I'd been into – big and small – had been in the country and of rustic style.

'Oh, 'tis all for show!' she said. 'They never come into these rooms. But you should see the bedrooms! The mistress's room has Venetian mirrors all over, and she sleeps in a four-poster with gold hangings that are said to have come from Persia.'

Once she'd told me this, I longed to go upstairs and

see these things, but Abby said she didn't dare take me. She did say, though, that if I went up the servants' stairs to her room, then she would go to the nursery and bring the babe to see me.

To tell the truth I was not that bothered about the babe, having seen more than enough of my little brothers and sisters as infants, but Abby said it was a pretty one and seemed so eager to show it off that we went to her room and I waited while she fetched it.

It *was* a pretty babe, about three months old and still swaddled, with thick dark hair. She was awake and smiled up at us, so Abby loosened the cambric sheet around her and let her wave her arms.

'This is Grace,' Abby said. 'And she must think I'm her mother, for it's been me who's been looking after her since she was born.'

'How is she fed if your mistress is so ill?' I asked. 'Does she have a wet nurse?'

Abby shook her head. 'They won't allow a wet nurse for fear of contagion, so a maid with the milch-ass calls here twice a day.' She stroked the baby's cheek. 'I trickle the milk down my hand and this little squab sucks my fingers.'

I was silent for a moment, and then I asked in a low voice, 'It's not plague that your mistress has, is it?'

Abby laughed. ''Tis not! Plague would have carried her off by now. It's just childbed fever. Though, to tell the truth,' she added, 'when I wash her, I always look her over for the tokens, for I know that plague is no respecter of persons. It can visit a lady as quick as an ale-house wife.'

'And do you take a preventative yourself?'

She nodded. 'The mistress's doctor made us up

some treacle with conserves of roses before he went into the country. And we all chew a piece of angelica root when we go out.'

Talking of the preventatives made me think of Tom, and, rather embarrassed, I brought his name into the conversation and asked Abby whether I should allow him the liberty of kissing me or not. 'I mean proper kissing – on the lips,' I explained.

She laughed. 'Of course!' she said. 'For what's a sweetheart for if you don't get one or two kisses from him!'

'Mother used to say—'

Abby waved her hand dismissively. 'It's different in London,' she said. 'And different now, when no one can count on living two days at a time. If you're visited by the plague—'

I gave a little gasp of fright.

'You don't want to go to your grave unkissed, do you?'

I smiled and blushed. 'Indeed I don't!'

'Well, then,' she said.

Laughing, I said I would think on it, and bid her goodbye.

Chapter Nine

The first week of August

*'And I frighted to see so many graves lie so high upon
the churchyard where so many have been buried of
the Plague.'*

'Praying is all very well,' said the stout woman in
church, 'but I cannot fast! And I do not see why I have
to. I don't believe the king will be fasting. I'm sure he
and his court will be sitting down to their grouse and
oysters and lobsters and geese just the same as they
always do!'

Sarah and I smiled at the woman, who was as wide
as she was high, and moved slightly further down the
pew and away from her. She was hot and red-faced
and we did not wish her breath to fall on us, for the
latest rumour was that you should keep cool and keep
your distance from others as much as possible in order
to avoid contaminated air. It appeared that the
authorities did not know this rumour, however, for we
were still required to attend church regularly, and
without fail on the first Wednesday in each month.

The Bills had shown that near two and a half thousand had died of plague in the past week, and on the way into St Dominic's that morning I had not been able to avoid seeing how the ground in the graveyard had risen; how corpses had been laid upon corpses so that the ground on each side of the pathway had swelled to a height of several feet. It made me shudder to see it, for I could not help but imagine them all lying there in the cold earth in their winding sheets – for few were given the sanctity of a coffin – old piled upon young, men upon women, laid without care or ceremony.

Once seated in church, we discovered that our own minister had moved to the safety of the country, and another now stood in his place. He gave a violent and frightening sermon which lasted nearly two hours, telling us that the plague was a judgement on the behaviour of the people, and of the terrible death and hellfire which awaited us unless we truly repented of our blasphemies and sins. He affrighted me so terribly that I had to take Sarah's hand, but she whispered to me that he could not mean the likes of us, for a just God could not account any sins *we* had committed as being evil enough to take us to Hell.

Going home, we saw a sad sight: a young woman carrying a small box in her arms, weeping aloud and calling, 'Oh my child . . . oh my precious!' as she trudged towards St Olave's churchyard. Sarah whispered that she probably wanted to take the baby to the graveyard herself and make sure it had a decent burial. 'For she will surely be shut in as soon as the authorities find out the child has died,' she added.

Another strange sight we saw was that of a poor

madman, raving deliriously, clad with only a cloth about his loins. He was beating his naked breast and screaming out to the Heavens to deliver him from his life on earth, for his whole family had been taken with the plague and he no longer wished to live. Sarah threw a coin to him and we hurried past without speaking.

When we got home, we found that a letter we had tried to send to our family telling them that all was well with us, had been returned undelivered. A man from the carriers told us that, despite this letter being steamed over a pot of boiling vinegar to kill any contagion, the authorities in Chertsey had refused to accept it. He said that many towns were no longer taking letters from London unless they concerned official business, or were a matter of life or death.

'Do you suppose they will know in Chertsey that the plague is upon us?' I asked Sarah.

'They are sure to,' she nodded. 'And Mother will be worried, no doubt. But they will think no news is good news.'

We changed out of our church-going clothes and, both being very hungry – for we had not yet broken our fast – we ate some of our sweetmeats. Sarah said it could not count as proper eating just to sample the stock, and besides, we had been left with rather a lot of crystallised violet and rose petals of late, because our trade had fallen off so much.

'To be plain, I am worried,' Sarah said. 'Our takings are down to less than a half of what they usually are.'

I was rather distracted, for I'd finished my violets and was looking at myself in a little mirror that I'd bought from a pedlar. It seemed to me that, despite all my efforts, my hair was wilder and curled more than ever.

'Hannah!' Sarah said. 'Did you hear me? With more and more of the quality going out of town, I fear we will soon not be making enough money to buy our daily food.'

'There won't be food to buy anyway, will there?' I said, putting the mirror away. 'Half the shops are already shut, and if it gets any worse Mr Newbery says we'll all starve!'

Sarah shook her head. 'We will not,' she said, 'for I have heard today of where we may buy provisions.'

'Where did you hear that?'

'While we were waiting to go into church this morning and you were staring at the graves and thinking of God knows what horrors, I was speaking to a man who lives near Lincolns Inn. We talked of the difficulty of getting food and he said that there are some country wives who are not willing to come into the city for fear of contagion, but who bring their wares to town and set them up for sale by the city gates. They bring rabbits and chickens and all manner of pies, and they are there every day of the week.'

'And we will always be able to get bread – so we will not starve after all!' I said.

Sarah shook her head. 'No, indeed. But about our trade. How can we sell more sweetmeats?'

We both fell to thinking.

'I could go out with a tray,' I said, and at Sarah's frown, added, 'Indeed I would not mind a bit.'

Sarah shook her head. 'I don't think it would be wise for you to walk the streets any more than you have to.' She thought some more. 'If we could make something which the poorer people needed, then we wouldn't worry about the quality going out of town.'

And then I thought of the answer. 'We must make sweetmeats which prevent the plague!' I cried.

Sarah clapped her hands. 'The very thing! Why didn't we think of it before?'

'We must look through our recipes and see what seeds and herbs are of most use,' I said, then hesitated. 'But how do we know anything will truly work against the sickness? How can we say what will work more than any other thing? Won't we be just like the quack doctors who set up stalls overnight and sell pellets of stale bread and call them plague pills?'

Sarah shook her head. 'There are a hundred different preventions now, and who is to say what works and what doesn't? Even the real doctors and apothecaries – even Doctor da Silva – don't know for certain what is of use.'

I nodded slowly. 'We may make the very things which make a difference.'

'We will make sugared comfits from the little spikes of rosemary! Everyone says rosemary is most efficacious.'

'And it will cost almost nothing, as we have a bush of it just outside our back door,' I said.

We sat and thought for a while, and looked through some of our aunt's papers, and in the end I went to see Tom at the apothecary's, for I assured Sarah that he would know as well as anyone what would be the best plants to use.

To my regret, Tom was not there, having apparently gone to the docks to fetch some very rare mineral compound. Doctor da Silva, who was boiling herbs in a pot, assured me, however, that rosemary comfits would be beneficial.

'And even if not beneficial, at least not harmful,' he added.

'And what else could we make into sweetmeats?'

'What of angelica? This is a most powerful herb of the sun in Leo and it would be right to gather it now.'

I nodded eagerly. 'We can candy the stems of angelica into sugar sticks.'

'And chervil has a root similar to that of angelica,' the doctor went on thoughtfully, 'and is said to be as effective, and there is also dragon-wort, which expels the venom of plague – although you may not know where to find it at this time of the year. The root of the scabious boiled in wine is a very powerful antidote, although I do not know how you would convert this into a sweetmeat.'

'But rosemary, angelica and chervil,' I said thoughtfully, 'we can use all these.' I spoke slowly, looking around the shelves of the shop, at the dusty bottles and phials, and hoping that Tom would arrive back before I left.

'And the flowers of garlic may also be candied,' the doctor said. 'Garlic is an efficacious remedy for all diseases.'

Some more customers arrived to see the doctor then, and feeling obliged to go home, I bobbed the doctor a curtsey and thanked him for his trouble.

''Tis nothing. We must all help each other in our distress,' the doctor said, and as I went to the door, added, 'Oh, by the way, some young ladies swear that an ointment made from cowslips rids them of their freckles.'

I was tempted to ask further, but as I did not wish to be thought of as an empty-headed baggage, I just said, 'When we are over our troubles, perhaps,' and asked him to please commend me to Tom.

Two days later, Sarah and I rose at the call of five o'clock, for we were going out to see if we could find angelica growing on the marshes. I had washed and left my washing water ready for Sarah – for it was not at all dirty – when she suddenly cried out my name in a most despairing voice.

I looked round, alarmed, and she was sitting on our bed in her shift, her face flushed and a hand pressed against her jaw. I immediately began to shake with fright, for I knew what must have happened: *She had found some swelling . . .*

I crouched down beside her. 'What is it?' I asked her urgently. 'Is it a lump?'

'I believe so,' she said shakily, feeling along her face. 'Just here.' She took my fingers and pressed them against her face, although – God forgive me – for an instant I wanted to recoil and snatch them back. 'Can you feel it too?'

I felt along the line of her jaw. 'I . . . I think so,' I said.

'There is pain, too, all down the side of my neck. And it has been so all night.'

'And on the other side?'

'Nothing.'

'Do you have any other symptoms?' I asked, my voice trembling. 'Fever? Do you feel sick? Have the giddiness? Do you have a headache?'

She shook her head to all of these except the last.

'Let's go quickly to Doctor da Silva, then,' I said, and she nodded speechlessly, her face as white as her shift.

While we dressed my mind was whirling ahead of me. If it indeed *was* plague, then without more ado we would be shut up in the house with a brutal minder at our door. I would have the same symptoms in one or two days, then Sarah would die, and I would follow. Mother and Father would find out in a letter from someone – a minister at the church, perhaps – and would come to London, but would be unable to find our grave.

And I would die unkissed, before I had hardly lived.

To our great relief the shop was open and the doctor was in, although it was his consultancy morning and there was a queue of people outside waiting to see him. They were going in one by one and talking to him privately, so we waited our turn, keeping our thoughts to ourselves and staying a good distance from everyone else. Indeed, some of them looked most alarming: one woman was greasy with sweat and moaning softly under her breath, and a man was naked to the waist, with great open wounds under his arm and on his chest. They were most gruesome to look upon, and I averted my eyes. Sarah whispered to me to keep away, for they were plague sores which had burst, and the man must be attending the doctor for healing herbs to be packed into the wounds.

It was Tom who opened the door to us, and when he saw it was me and Sarah waiting to see the doctor a look of such horror crossed his face that it almost brought tears to my eyes, for I knew then how he felt about me, and that it was the same as the way I felt about him.

This was some small comfort to me for my mind was a perfect blank of dread. I began to pray, something I had not done properly, really meaning it, for many a month. I began to make God any number of entreaties and promises if only he would make Sarah well again.

I had already told Sarah of Doctor da Silva's strange outfit, so she was not too shocked when our turn came. We were led behind a screen and she saw him sitting there with his bird's head, his breath rasping through the beak of herbs.

'I have a . . . a lump,' Sarah stammered. 'Here.' She took off her cap and lifted her head, turning her face slightly so that he could see it more clearly. 'It's very painful,' she said.

The doctor lifted a candle high and looked at the swelling, which to my eyes seemed to have grown since we left home. He pressed it with his fingers, and Sarah winced, then he directed her to open her mouth and probed inside with a small wooden stick.

'Is it plague?' I asked fearfully, begging God to spare her. 'What can you tell?'

The doctor pulled off his beak headgear and put on his glasses, then he looked in Sarah's mouth again. He smiled – a smile most delightful for us to see. 'It is a tooth in your lower jaw,' he said. 'It has an abscess underneath which is full of poison, and this is what is swelling your gum.'

Tears began to swim in Sarah's eyes and, seeing them, my eyes filled too. 'Are you sure?' she asked.

'I am indeed!' said the doctor, 'and happy to be so.'

He reached behind him for a small bottle. 'I will rub some oil of cloves on it, and Tom will give you a root of saxifrage to chew if the pain gets too much. But you must go and get it pulled.'

'Can you not do that?' I asked.

He shook his head. 'But there is a man who pulls teeth at the sign of the Red Bull, by the coffee shop in Covent Garden. He wields a fair instrument.' He gave Sarah an awkward pat on the shoulder. 'I am glad to have given you good news.'

'We . . . we must pay you,' she stammered.

He shook his head. 'No need. Instead, Tom and I will have some of your fine new sweetmeats against plague.'

Tom had heard everything and was smiling fit to burst when we came around the screen. He gave us a piece of dried root of saxifrage and explained again exactly where the man who drew teeth was to be found, then opened the door so that we could be released and the next poor customer could enter.

The feeling I had on walking home was one of such joy and relief that I felt I wanted to dance and sing aloud, and without thinking I began to hum a tune I'd heard the balladeers singing, linking arms with Sarah and swaying with her. My poor sister, though, was still in some pain and said to me quietly, 'The plague is still around, Hannah. We are not through it yet. We must still be vigilant.'

I stopped humming and swaying when she said this, for indeed I had heard – could always hear – the bells of many different churches tolling for more deaths.

Sarah, being very frightened of the tooth-puller,

waited to see if the medicaments that the doctor had prescribed had any effect. They worked but a little, though, so at noon we went down to Covent Garden and found the tooth-puller at his booth by the sign of the Red Bull, and indeed we did not have to hunt for him, for the fellow – a man as big and as sweaty as an ox – was waving a frightening instrument in his hand and calling at the very pitch of his voice that he cut out ulcers, drew wormy teeth and lanced boils in the mouth.

Sarah hung back when she saw him. 'He looks a dirty and ignorant fellow,' she whispered.

'But the doctor recommended him,' I reminded her. I held her hand and led her towards him. 'And it will be over in a minute and then you can forget all about it.'

The man sat her on a little stool, bent her head back and pushed his fingers into her mouth so she had no choice but to open it widely. He looked at her gum, then he unclipped some pincers from his belt and thrust them in her mouth so that her face twisted into a strange shape. He fitted the pincers on to the tooth and pulled. There was a gurgled scream from Sarah and she squeezed my hand so tightly I swear she almost broke my fingers. Then, suddenly, he was holding the tooth aloft and proclaiming himself the fastest tooth-drawer in the city.

Sarah was pale and trembling all over, so I paid the fellow and we went home, only stopping on the way to buy an infusion of blackberry flowers and leaves to help heal her mouth. Sarah then went to bed and slept most of the rest of the day, while I opened the shop (but sold little) and amused myself by finding a stub of pencil and making a list of what sweetmeats we were going to make and the ingredients we would need to buy for our new undertaking. I was reasonably content as I did this, for I knew Sarah would be well, I had Tom to think on, and – apart from losing dearest Mew – all was well with us.

That night, though, I heard it for the first time.

The plague cart.

There came the noise of wheels trundling on cobblestones and I went to the shutters to look out, for lately there had scarce been any traffic by our door.

What I saw was a big farm cart, like the one I'd ridden on to London with Farmer Price. At the front sat two men, gruesome-looking ruffians, unhatted, wearing long black coats, and holding flaming torches aloft in the darkness. Instead of their load being hay, the harvest they carried was bodies: about twenty of them, wrapped in winding sheets or tied into knotted shrouds, two or three of them stark naked, their limbs gleaming pale under the light from the torches.

'Bring out your dead!' they cried, ringing a bell. 'Bring out your dead!'

As I looked on, horrified, a door opened in one of the houses opposite and an old man called to the drivers. One of them then went to the door of the house with what looked like a shepherd's crook in his hand and, taking a step inside, he thrust in the hooked part and dragged out the body of an old woman wearing a nightshirt. This tumbled down the doorstep and on to the ground, prompting a cry of despair from the old man.

The back of the cart was let down and the men

manipulated the body with their crooks, throwing it all anyhow on to the cart, so that the poor corpse's long grey hair tumbled to her shoulders and her nightshirt came up, exposing her white and wizened limbs to the world.

Without another word to the one who stood alone on the doorstep, the men stowed their hooks, got up on their seats and drove off. I watched their progress down the street, listening to the cry of, 'Bring out your dead!' until the words and the sound of the cart wheels were too far off to be heard.

When I crept back to bed I longed to wake Sarah, wanting to share with someone the awful sight I'd seen. I did not, however, feeling that she'd been upset enough that day. Instead, I laid in the darkness, going over what I'd seen and seeming to feel within me a thousand dormant symptoms of plague stirring into life. Would we survive?

Why should we when so many others were dying?

How cheap life seemed. How random.

Bring out your dead . . . The words echoed around my head until dawn.

Chapter Ten

The second week of August

'The people die so, that now it seems they are fain to carry the dead to be buried by daylight, the nights not sufficing to do it.'

We had managed to get all the ingredients we needed for our new venture, and were now selling sugared chips of angelica and chervil, herb comfits containing leaves of rosemary and caraway seeds, and candied garlic and rosemary flowers. We had also prepared lozenges from rue which we had chopped with caraway seeds and mixed with sugar and rose water. Although we had not been told that this herb, rue, was a plague preventative, its old name was herb of grace, and Sarah felt that anything with that name was sure to be beneficial. Besides, a green man had called at our door selling flowers and herbs, and he had given us a large bunch of rue very cheaply.

I had prepared a notice to go outside the shop which advertised our new produce. In order to help our customers who could not read I had merely written the word PLAGUE and drawn a cross through it, for now all, even the most ignorant, knew that dread word by sight. For those who could read I gave more information.

Excellent electuaries against the Plague may be bought at the sign of the Sugared Plum.

When you go abroad, chew the sugared root of Angelica or the herb, Rosemary.

Also take our lozenges made with the ancient Herb of Grace.

I had copied some of these words from bills I had seen posted on tavern walls and windows, and I was very pleased with the result.

Even though the streets seemed thin of people, within three days we had sold out of everything we had made and had to prepare more. One of our customers – a proper gentleman, with velvet and gold-laced jacket and long curled wig – told us that he had never found the taking of medicine more delightful than when it was coated with sugar candy.

'And never has it been served by two more delightful gals,' he added, chucking me under the chin and giving me an extra twopence when he handed me his payment. I could see by the look in his eye that, given any encouragement, he would have come round the counter and put his arm about my waist, so I merely dropped my eyes and thanked him demurely.

Scowling at his departing back, I asked Sarah who he was.

'Someone at the Admiralty,' she said. 'I forget his name. Someone very high up, I believe.'

Soon after his visit, Mr Newbery came in to buy some lozenges from us.

'For I've heard that these are very tasty and strong,' he said, and I assured him that indeed they were, and that they had been praised highly by members of the Admiralty.

Sarah came through from the back and asked if he knew what the Bills were for that week.

'I do, and I wish I didn't,' Mr Newbery said, 'for they are three thousand!' As Sarah and I gasped, he added, 'Three thousand – with another thousand of what they call "other causes".'

Sarah shook her head worriedly. 'The plague is now in every parish of London, I have heard.'

'That's true. And I have heard that there are five plague pits dug to accommodate its victims.'

'We have heard of them – have you seen one?' I asked Mr Newbery. 'I did wonder how . . . how big they are.'

'Hannah!' Sarah rebuked me.

'For I cannot imagine . . .' my voice trailed away. We had heard reports of these pits which had had to be dug because the churchyards could not take any more corpses. Rumours said that they were vast holes that held forty . . . sixty . . . eighty bodies or more.

'I have heard that the biggest can hold two hundred!' Mr Newbery said. 'They are dug as deep as a man can stand in the ground, and can be as wide as the church of St Paul's. They are needed, too, for I have heard that in some parishes the death cart is coming by day now as well as by night, for the hours of darkness are not enough to take all the corpses.'

Sarah went through to our back room, shooting me a glance which meant we had heard enough of such matters.

'But have you heard about the piper?' Mr Newbery asked, and I shook my head.

Mr Newbery popped a comfit into his mouth. 'Well, they do say that a piper – just a common music man – fell down in the street insensible with drink. In the night the plague cart came round and thinking he had been struck dead, hooked him up and threw him on to a cart already piled with bodies. He was buried under more, but the jolting of the cart woke him just as they reached the pit, and he sat upright and began playing his pipes to draw attention to his plight.'

Mr Newbery paused to suck noisily on the comfit. 'The drivers of the cart couldn't see him in the dark, just heard uncanny music coming from the load of bodies, and they bolted in terrible fright, saying that they had taken up the Devil himself on to their cart!' He laughed. 'Now, what think you of that?'

I smiled, although in truth I did not know whether to laugh or cry.

'Truly, the spectre of death stares each of us in the face!' Mr Newbery said cheerfully as he went out.

That night I had a terrible nightmare. I was alive, but lying in a plague pit under a press of bodies which weighed down on me so that I could neither move nor hardly breathe. Something – some foul-smelling piece of dead flesh – was hard against my mouth and my hair was held knotted in a dead man's grip so I could not change the angle of my head to enable me to gather my strength and scream. I had no way of knowing how far down the pile of corpses I was and knew I would suffocate unless I could claw my way through them and reach the top of the heap.

My nightmare was ended when I kicked out and hit Sarah in my efforts to climb, and she woke me properly by shaking my shoulder and calling my name. She went back to sleep quickly but I lay awake for an age, wishing I could feel the comfort of Mew's little body on my feet and wondering when the Bills would show a downturn and we could go back to living an ordinary life.

The next morning Abby came round to purchase some sweetmeats, saying that her mistress had a fancy for something light and delicate to tempt her appetite. We had no crystallised violets or rose petals now, but instead gave her some candied angelica and also some citron chips made from an orange, which Sarah said was held to be good for an invalid, and which we had made the same way as the angelica chips by boiling three times in sugared water.

Abby had a pomander of herbs and flowers which she sniffed constantly as she spoke to us, and she had also tucked some blue flowers behind her ear. She said they were cornflowers and she was wearing them as a plague prevention, but indeed they looked so fetching – the blue against her dark curls – that I resolved that I too would obtain and wear some.

We gossiped at the door while Sarah was weighing up the citron chips, finding it strange that we could now look up and down the street with hardly anything to spoil our view, for as well as being quiet of people and their conveyances, there were no cats, dogs, pigs or goats around either. Indeed, there had been so little traffic that grass and weeds had started to sprout between the cobblestones.

'Your mistress is still not well enough to travel?' I asked Abby.

She shook her head. 'She's improving, but she dreads the length of the journey and the battering and jolting our bodies must take on the way.' She looked up and down the street. 'Are you all in good health here? Praise be, I don't see many shut-up houses in view.'

'There are two newly shut just around the corner,' I said. 'And a woman who was a customer of ours has this morning been taken to a pesthouse.'

Abby shook her head. 'I went past the Exchange just now and when I looked in there was scarce anyone there. And no one of quality at all.'

Before I could comment on this she said, 'And what do you think – our cook was on a ferry going across to Southwarke when the boatman was suddenly struck blind and dumb!'

'And then what happened?' I asked, alarmed.

'Well, the boat started drifting downstream and one of the men passengers had to push the boatman to one side, take the oars and carry on rowing across.'

'Did they reach the other side? What of the ferryman?' I asked.

'By the time they got to the other side, he was dead! And he had the tokens on him in a ring around his neck, though everyone swore they were not there when they got on board, or they surely would not have gone with him.'

'Abby's sweetmeats are wrapped and ready!' Sarah called from inside the shop, but I pretended not to hear her. She was always telling me not to listen to gossip, that it made one morbid, but I took little heed.

'But is your cook all right?' I asked Abby.

Abby nodded. 'Fat and healthy as ever was a sow. But did you hear of the wraith in the woods?'

I shook my head and asked Abby to tell me straightaway, for despite being in dread of what I might hear, I could not bear *not* to know. 'A real wraith – you mean, a ghost creature?' I asked.

'It happened outside the city,' Abby said in a low, storytelling voice. 'At Brentwood, I believe. A maid in a big house had been taken ill of the plague and was removed to a shed in the garden to be away from the family. A nurse who was appointed to look after her went to get some medicines, and while she was gone the maid escaped from a window. When the nurse returned she got no answer to her knocks and, believing her patient to be dead, told the master of the house so.'

She paused for breath and I urged her to go on quickly, fearing that Sarah would come up any minute and I would not hear the end of the tale.

'Well, the master was much disturbed, for none of the villagers would touch a plague victim to bury them, so he went into Brentwood to obtain assistance in getting rid of the corpse. On his way back through the woods, though, he encountered the maid and believing it to be her wraith, ran back home, shouting and raving mad. Finally, it was discovered that the maid had got out of the shed window, then she was found in the woods and put into a cart to be carried off to a pesthouse.'

I gasped. 'And did the master of the house recover from his madness?'

Abby looked surprised. 'I do not know!' she said.

Chapter Eleven

The third week of August

'And my Lord Mayor commands people to be within at nine at night that the sick may have liberty to go abroad for air.'

For the next few days we were very busy, for news of our plague prevention sweetmeats was spreading and they were selling well, which caused us to be up all hours making more. I did not see Tom but I thought of him often – especially when I took the cordial he had made – and wondered how long it would be before I set eyes on him. I thought too about our first kiss, and could hardly wait for it.

On Friday evening I was putting up the shutters outside the shop when a lad came running down the road looking about him in a distracted way, studying the signs as if he was looking for one in particular.

As he came closer I saw to my surprise that it was the boy groom at the house where Abby was in service. Suddenly spotting our sign, he made a lunge towards me.

'The sign of the Sugared Plum! You're Hannah?' he asked, panting.

I nodded, rather intrigued, wondering what he could want.

'I have a message from Abby.' He doubled up then, breathless from running, and tried to regain breath enough to speak.

'Is it your mistress? Does she want more sweetmeats?' I asked, thinking to help.

'No – it's our house!' the boy croaked. 'Our house has been enclosed.'

I gasped and stepped backwards. 'It has been visited with plague?'

He nodded.

'And is it Abby who is sick?' I asked fearfully, and while I was anxious for my friend I was also terrified for myself, trying to think how close we had stood while she'd been telling me about the wraith, and whether or not she might have passed on any contagion to me.

He shook his head. 'It's Cook,' he said. 'Cook was taken very sick last night and a doctor came and said it's plague and we all have to be shut up.'

'But *you're* not shut up.'

'I ran off – and one of the maids got out as well. But Abby shouted down to ask me to come and tell you what had happened.'

Shakily, I asked who was left in the house, and he told me his master, mistress, the housekeeper, cook, two maids, and the babe.

'But is Abby well?' I asked anxiously.

He nodded. 'As well as anyone can be knowing they're going to be locked up for forty days,' he said.

'And your master and mistress?'

'Everyone is well except the cook, who is of a fearsome waxwork complexion and everyone says is like to die at any minute.'

I moved myself just a little further off. 'But where will you go now?'

'I will try and get back to my family in Suffolk,' the boy said.

'You don't have a Certificate of Health.'

He shook his head. 'I'll go across country and no one will see me. I'll sleep in barns and under hedges and get a message to my ma somehow so that she will send a cart out for me.'

I looked at him with concern. 'I wish you well, then.'

He grinned at me, not seeming to realise the seriousness of his situation. 'Abby said you would give me something for my trouble in coming here.'

I nodded, went inside and got him a few pennies, and also gave him a hunk of bread and some cherries.

While he ate the cherries he told me that there was now a guard outside the house, but if I went round to the back yard and called up, then Abby would come and speak to me out of the first-floor window. He bade me go there as quickly as possible, and then he stuffed the piece of bread inside his shirt and ran off, leaving me to go inside and tell Sarah this news.

I thought at first that Sarah would raise some objections to my going to see Abby, but she did not, for she had known her and her family as long as I had and was equally anxious to know that she was all right. I was not frightened, for I felt there would be no risk in speaking to Abby from the distance of a window. Just as soon as we had eaten supper, I set off.

The streets were quiet as I hurried along, not looking at anyone nor acknowledging those who might be looking at me. When I got to City Road someone hailed me and shouted that I should go home, but I thought it was just a madman and did not take any notice. A little further on, however, I chanced upon a crier in a square who was ringing his bell and calling nine of the clock as being an hour of curfew. At this time, he called, all able-bodied people were to stay inside their houses and allow those who had been visited by plague to walk the streets and take the air unimpeded.

I panicked then, for of course I had not known about this curfew and immediately visualised a vast crowd of diseased people sweeping through the streets and infecting me with their weeping sores and foetid breath. I turned to go home and, thinking to take a short cut, went down a long, narrow alley. When I emerged I did not know where I was and, the sun having gone down, could not work out in which direction to walk.

I turned to the right but when I reached the Fleet River I knew immediately that I was not going in the proper direction, and turned back. In my haste, however, I missed the alley through which I had come. Breaking into a run, I at length found myself close to the city walls and near the church of St Just. I did not wish to approach the only person who passed, who had his eyes and hands raised to heaven and was praying aloud for God to have mercy on us all, so thought it best to go towards the church and hope to see someone of authority there to ask for directions.

Alas, I could see no minister but, instead, beyond the church my eyes seized upon the most dreadful sight: one of the plague pits that Mr Newbery had spoken of, a cavernous black hole in the ground, lit by the flares and torches of those standing nearby. There were some men inside the pit itself, walking about (perhaps on bodies, I thought), and some more men beside a plague cart which had just pulled up.

This cart was pulled by drayhorses and contained a stack of dead bodies, perhaps thirty or forty of them. I could not help but watch as it tipped up and the pile of bodies tumbled into the pit, a jumbled heap of limbs, hair and rags.

'Here's another load of faggots!' I heard a man call, and there was a roar of laughter.

'Pile 'em in and pile 'em up!' another shouted.

As I watched, the men already in the pit moved across and poked and hooked the corpses so they laid at an even level, and others shook out lime from great sacks and strewed it over them. I did not hear one murmured prayer or exclamation of sorrow, and indeed all was conducted with a callous and cruel indifference to the poor corpses which were now spread out before them all.

As another plague cart arrived I turned away, sickened to my very heart, and by sheer good fortune managed to find the right path home. The horror of that evening was not yet over, though, because on the way back I encountered the dead body of a young man propped in a doorway. He held a Bible in his hands and his eyes were wide open and staring. The sight of him gave me the most dreadful fright.

I arrived home before the plague victims walked

out, however, and after thoroughly washing myself (for I felt clammy and dirty from all I had seen) Sarah and I waited for these poor creatures to appear, watching with a morbid curiosity from behind our shutters. The streets were completely deserted now and it was as silent as a morgue outside, apart from the far-off tolling of a bell, when some tapping and shuffling noises were heard along the cobblestones.

We were expecting to see fearsome monsters, but when the sufferers came into view they were not monsters at all, just a straggling line of pitiful creatures: old and young, stooped and upright, ugly and fair, some recovering from the sickness and walking with an almost confident stride, some bent almost double and held up with sticks, and one or two pushed in a cart by others. The one thing they had in common was that they were all plague sufferers – and wore stained and tattered bandages as their mark of distinction.

'And these are just the ones who are well enough to come out,' Sarah breathed as we watched the pathetic procession pass our shop.

Perhaps forty passed in ones and twos, some carrying flares before them, and then a party from a pesthouse came along together: ten or twelve led by a surly-looking nurse, all carrying white staves in front of them. I imagined them returning to the pesthouse and telling the inmates who had not been well enough to walk of the things they'd seen, of a strange London, shut up and unearthly quiet, seemingly populated by none but plague victims.

I went to sleep that night worried because I had not been able to speak to Abby, and Sarah said I should go first thing the following morning.

In the morning Mr Newbery was standing outside his shop telling early passers-by that four and a half thousand had died of plague that week, and making much of a tale he'd heard of one of the plague walkers of the previous night who'd dropped down dead just outside St Saviour's.

'He was a frowsy-headed old man, rich with lice,' he said, 'and when he dropped to the ground, those coming after threw him over the wall into the churchyard. They just picked him up and chucked him over like a bundle of sticks!'

I made noises of surprise and disgust.

'Well, it saved the cart coming!' Mr Newbery said. He scratched his fat belly. 'But where are you heading so early on this hot morning?' he asked, and I told him the truth: that I was going to see my friend Abby, who'd recently been enclosed.

He stepped back from me and crossed himself, looking at me in alarm. 'Those enclosed are fuel for the carts,' he said. 'She'll not make old bones!'

I was about to make a witty return, for I'd found that this was the only way to deal with Mr Newbery, but to my horror I found my eyes filling with tears. I turned away, saying nothing.

I found London very different that day, perhaps because something had happened which touched me personally. The sun still shone but it seemed to have drained the colour from the City, for the house signs no longer glittered and the people (what few there were abroad, and none in the bright colours that denoted them to be of quality) were slow and dull of spirit, going about their business with their eyes cast down and none of their usual laughter or banter. The houses were desolate, too. Amid those that had crosses on their doors were many which had been deserted by their owners. They stood empty and lifeless, having been cleared of anything of value and boarded up. I missed the animals, too: the pink grunting pigs, the fighting dogs and the cats which had silently slipped in and out of the shadows. Their robust farmyard smell had disappeared and been replaced by an unwholesome and putrid stink which those such as Doctor da Silva called a *miasma*: a sickening, invisible fog emanating from the graveyards which were now choked with rotting bodies.

When I arrived at the front of Abby's house I saw a most fearsome sight, for the plague cart was at the front door and the carters were taking away a large bundle. Of course, my first fear was that it was Abby, for notwithstanding that the groom had told me last night that she was perfectly healthy, I had heard many tales of persons being well one moment and dead the next.

I held back for a while in the shadow of the opposite building, my heart pounding, but then, having judged by the size of the corpse that it could not be Abby, went around the back of the house to call up to her.

She was already at the first-floor window, standing looking out with the babe in her arms, and she looked so thankful to see me that I almost fell to crying. She still had a flower tucked behind her ear, but that flower was fading now, and her face was pale, her dress creased and stained.

'I have been here since daylight,' she said and, when I began to apologize for not getting there earlier, added that it was not because she was especially waiting for me, but because she wished little Grace to draw in what fresh air she could from outside and not let her breathe in the foul atmosphere of the house.

'I saw the cart outside,' I said. 'Who was it that died?'

'Cook,' she answered.

'So quickly?' I gasped.

She nodded. 'I did not like the old baggage . . .' Here she stopped and struggled to compose herself. '. . . but I would not have wished that death on her.'

'How did she . . . did she have the buboes?'

Abby nodded. 'In her groin. She screamed for four hours last night.'

'Was there nothing could be done?'

'Nothing. She cried out that she could not bear the pain and was going to fling herself out of the window, and the nurse had to tie her to her bed.'

I shuddered. 'And then what—?'

'Then she fell into a deep sleep and woke before dawn to start screaming again. She found the strength from somewhere to break the ropes that bound her, then ran through the house and threw herself down the back staircase.' Abby drew in a little breath, making a sound between a sob and a laugh. 'She knew her place even then, see, for she made sure it was the servants' stairs.'

She dipped her head and wiped her eyes on the swaddling sheet. 'And now her neck is broke and she is no more.'

'And you. Are . . . are you well?' I faltered.

132

She struggled to compose herself. 'I am. I'll be all right. For aren't we good country stock and as strong as 'roaches?' She smiled faintly.

'And what of the others in the house?'

'The master complains that he cannot sleep for pains in his arms, so they are going to send the doctor round,' Abby said. 'And one of the maids says she has a sick headache. But every little sniff and ache is the plague to us!'

'Is there anything you want?'

She shook her head. 'The milch-ass comes twice a day, an apothecary calls with fresh tinctures and the wretch at the door buys our food for us. We have everything we need.' She looked at me bleakly. 'We just have to wait.'

'Forty days?'

'Forty days from the last death,' Abby said wearily. 'If another of us dies in a week's time, or two weeks' time, then that forty days will start again.'

I swallowed and my throat was dry with horror, for I knew I could not bear being shut up in that house for those weeks amongst the dead and dying. 'I have brought you some sweetmeats,' I said quickly. 'Candied angelica and some rosemary comfits.'

Comfits for corpses. The thought came to me unbidden and I quickly brushed it aside.

Abby looked a little cheered. 'I will send down a basket,' she said, and holding the babe deftly in the crook of her arm, she put out a little wicker basket on a string and lowered it to the ground. Carefully – I did not let my fingers come into contact with the basket – I put the cones of sweetmeats in and stood back to allow her to pull it up.

'Will you come again, Hannah?' she asked.

I nodded. 'I will try to come every day. And if you need anything, you must tell me and I will try to get it for you.'

We blew kisses, said goodbye, and I turned away.

Abby called me back. 'Hannah!' she added, with a touch of her old spirit. 'You be sure to kiss your sweetheart!'

Chapter Twelve

The fourth week of August

*'Every day sadder and sadder news of its increase . . .
it is feared that the true number of the dead this week
is nearer ten thousand.'*

For the next few days the church bells seemed to toll
incessantly for one death after another, until an Order
came from the Lord Mayor that they should be
stopped, for everyone was much cast down by hearing
them. The weariness of spirit I'd noticed around me
when visiting Abby had spread and it seemed that
some people no longer cared what happened. This led
them to go one of two ways: either they sank into a
deep gloom, or they began frequenting the ale houses
(for these had begun to open again) and drank
themselves past false joviality and into a stupor.

Although our herbal sweetmeats were still selling
quite well, no one had much faith in preventatives any
more – not when the dead were to be found clutching
the very talismans that they'd hoped would save them.
There were no directives from the authorities and it

seemed that they had washed their hands of us, for the only new instruction we heard was that it was forbidden to build plague hospitals near to the dwellings of persons of substance and quality.

I had a mind to visit Abby again, but the next morning, after sleeping badly (for I still had the fear of the plague pit on me), I could hardly rouse myself up, and my legs trembled as I put them to the floor.

Sarah bade me stay in bed. 'For if you feel weak you may be more likely to take infection,' she said.

The next morning I was the same and I slept most of that day, weary, tearful and, for the first time, wishing myself safe back in Chertsey with my brothers and sisters. It crossed my mind – and of course it crossed Sarah's – that these were the first stirrings of plague about my body, but praise be, the third morning, I felt better and was anxious to go out and see how Abby fared.

Before I could do this, however, Mr Newbery came in to tell us a fresh and morbid tale, which was of a friend of his, one Josiah Brown, who, he said, was as well and as merry a chap as ever you could meet. 'He took all the precautions against the plague, and when he was out he carried a cloth of vinegar over his face, and never failed to change into fresh garments after going abroad. I saw him last week and he stood as healthy as you or I!' he said. 'Well, on Monday, my friend Josiah met someone in the street – an astrologer – who took one look and told him that he saw the mark of death on him.'

Sarah and I exchanged glances, knowing what was coming next.

'Why, Josiah laughed in his face,' Mr Newbery went

on, 'and said he had never felt so well in all his life. But when he got home he changed his clothes and saw to his horror that he had the tokens on his breast. And he knew that the tokens were gangrene spots and that the plague had gone inwards and mortified his flesh.' He paused for breath. 'And then my friend Josiah just sat down and died.'

Sarah tutted, shook her head, but I was silent, thinking of Abby.

'Eat, drink and be merry for tomorrow we die!' Mr Newbery went on. 'You may as well die happy as any other way.' He winked at me. 'Or catch the French pox, eh? That's worth a try!'

I didn't know what he was talking about but when he left, Sarah blushingly told me that it was thought that if a man lay with a prostitute and caught a disease, then that would stop him catching the plague. 'But 'tis all just a rumour,' she said, 'for no one knows anything of what is true and what is not any more.' She frowned. 'But I cannot believe that God would allow a man to be saved by sleeping with a . . . a whore, for this wouldn't be right.'

On the way to Abby's house, to my horror, I saw another corpse on the street (a woman, seemingly big with child) and heard the agonised sobs of people from an enclosed room, and so began to fear of what I might find when I reached Belle Vue House. But Abby was at the window once more, though looking pale and weary. There was no flower behind her ear now, and her hair was hanging in lank tails on each side of her face.

I asked how she was and she shook her head listlessly. 'I am well enough and I have no lumps,' she said, 'but I fear I shall go mad with being enclosed here.'

'But how is your mistress – and the babe?' I added anxiously, for I could see she was not nursing it as usual.

She shook her head. 'The babe is well and sleeps. But Mistress Beauchurch does nothing but cry and 'tis difficult to tell whether she is sick or well. My master has now a lump in his groin and groans aloud – I fear he is failing – and Becky, the other maid, lies in bed with such a sweat on her that we cannot keep her dry no matter how often we change the sheets.'

I gasped. 'Is it plague, then?'

Abby did not reply for a moment and I had to ask again.

'We fear so,' she then answered in a low voice. 'For she was often enough with Cook.'

'And do you have to nurse her?'

She shrugged. 'We have a nurse-minder sent in by the parish every morning, but she is a haggard old crone who knows next to nothing, and Becky is terrified of her.' Abby's hands gripped the sides of the window frame. 'Hannah, if I die you must promise you'll get a message to my mother in Chertsey.'

'Of course!' I said before I could stop myself, and quickly added, 'But you won't die! We're strong as 'roaches, remember?'

But her eyes had glazed over and she was thinking I knew not what terrible thoughts. I tried to think of things to speak about to lighten her heart, but it was hard, for all that was on my mind – indeed, all that was on the mind of anyone in London – was the plague, the pits, the corpses on the streets and horrid tales of those who had been afflicted. I left her, promising that I would go back as soon as I could, and I vowed to myself that I would do this even if I had the lethargy on me again, for it seemed little enough in comparison to what she was going through.

At home I had the most pleasant surprise, for Tom was there taking a glass of small beer with Sarah. She had sent a message to Doctor da Silva while I'd been out, to ask for something which would help me sleep soundly and prevent nightmares, and Tom had brought up a phial containing oil of lavender.

He told me to put one drop on my tongue on retiring, and one on my pillow.

'No more,' he said, 'for it is extremely potent.'

'And will it help her sleep?' Sarah asked him anxiously.

He nodded. 'It helps in all manner of night terrors and passions of the heart.' He smiled at me mischievously as he said these last four words, and raised his eyebrows. I could not help myself smiling back at him.

He could not stay, for at Doctor da Silva's they were busy day and night with making preventatives, for although it seemed that people no longer believed in them, they still wanted to take them.

'The doctor says they must have hope in something, for if that goes then all is lost,' Tom said, draining his glass.

He and I went to the door of the shop together and I told him the latest news about Abby and asked if he could offer any advice. He could not, however, apart from saying that I should tell Abby not to sleep in the same room as Becky, that she should keep to her own chamber as much as possible.

I hesitated before asking my next question. 'Do you think it is . . . is dangerous for me to speak to Abby from some distance away?'

He shook his head slowly. 'I do not think so,' he said. 'But no one knows for sure.' He took my hand and spoke earnestly to me, 'Hannah, you *will* take care, will you not?'

I nodded shyly.

'I think about you often, and if I could do what the necromancers say they can do, and cast a cloak of protection over you, then I would.'

Our gazes locked and I could not reply for the fullness of my heart and the tightness in my throat.

'And when all this is over . . .' he said softly.

Our hands touched, I lifted my face to his and let my eyelids drift down, ready . . . then I heard a jovial laugh beside us and Mr Newbery's voice saying, 'Ah, that's right – gather ye rosebuds while ye may!'

Unwillingly, I opened my eyes.

'That's what the poet tells us,' Mr Newbery went on, 'and in this dark time it would be as well to remember it!'

I glared at him, thinking that if ever there was an inappropriate time for Mr Newbery to appear with one of his stories, then this was it. But he did not seem to notice, just looked from me to Tom, casting his merry and unwelcome smile on each of us in turn. 'If I'm not mistaken, you're the 'prentice lad from the apothecary's!' he said. 'Now, tell me what faith you have in holding a gold angel in your mouth to keep off the sickness, for I have heard 'tis the very thing.'

Tom cast a sorry look at me, twining his hand in mine, and I squeezed his fingers for goodbye and dropped a small curtsey, for I knew Mr Newbery could speak for a great deal of time when he had a mind to.

'If you'll excuse me . . .' I murmured, and Tom smiled at me – a bright, tender smile – before I went inside again.

I used the lavender oil that night, and, thinking of Tom before I went to sleep, did sleep sounder and felt better. To my great shame, however, I let two whole days elapse before visiting Abby again. I had no excuse to offer for this, except my own selfishness, for while I stayed with Sarah and kept within the confines of the shop I felt I was out of harm's way. I did not feel safe in the city any more, for Death stalked its streets and no one was immune. I no longer thought London an exciting place to be.

Abby was not waiting at the window when I went round, nor did she come when I called up to her. I waited and called again, several times, and at length, fearing the very worst and chastising myself for staying away, I went round to the front of the house and spoke to the man guarding the door. At least there *was* a man still guarding them, I thought, so there must be someone alive inside.

I told him that I had come to speak to my friend the maid but had not been able to rouse her, and fearfully asked him if there had been other deaths in the house. He told me there had, but he could not say who they were.

'For the usual fellow is taken sick and I only came

here last night,' he said.

I began trembling, and felt ashamed and low, for what if Abby had died since my last visit . . . had dragged herself to the window to look for me, but I had not come?

'How many have died altogether in the house?' I asked.

He shrugged. 'Three, I believe. Or four.'

I went round to the back again and threw some gravel up to the window, and called and called. At last, at very long last, someone appeared. It was Abby, yet not the Abby I knew, for this person had a wild eye and a pain-filled face, and her forehead glittered with beads of sweat.

I could see at once that she had been deeply and fatally afflicted, but I tried to swallow down the fright I felt at her appearance. 'At last,' I said, 'I have been a-calling this hour or more.'

Abby smiled down at me. A strange smile she had, and an odd gleam in her eye.

'I have been visited, Hannah!' she said, and to my extreme surprise her voice had the tone of one telling another that a favourite friend had called. 'Visited at last. It courted me but I resisted it for days . . .'

'I . . . I see,' I said.

'Death called me to come into his arms! And what is a maid to do?' She gave a sudden cry of pain and clutched her head with both hands. 'Oh, but it is a hard and spiteful master!' she cried.

I choked back tears. 'Are you in great pain, Abby? Where is the nurse to look after you?'

'The nurse hasn't arrived today, Hannah. No nurse.' She shook her head gravely. 'She must be dead too.

They are all dead. And I have two fearful lumps come up in my groin so that I cannot walk as far as the privy but must lie in my own soil.'

I was sickened at this, but tried not to show it. Poor, poor Abby, who so loved her pretty gowns and her silk ribbons and who had come out with me on many a May morning in order to bathe her face in the dew and be beautiful.

'Is *everyone* dead, Abby? Your master and mistress too?'

She nodded. 'Within an hour of each other. In the beautiful chamber with the mirrors from Venice and the hangings from Persia.'

'But – *all* dead? What about the babe?'

'The babe!' A sudden light lit her face. 'Little Grace survives. But she cries – oh, how she cries! She is a poor orphan babe though, so she is right to cry.' Abby was leaning against the window frame and suddenly slipped sideways so that she disappeared from view. I called to her again.

'Abby!' I said urgently. 'What can I do for you? Is there something I can get you? Anything at all?'

I didn't think I would get a proper response, for I could see that the horror of what she must have seen in that house had already driven her half mad, but suddenly her two hands appeared, gripping the sill, and she pulled herself to her feet.

She looked at me with glittering eyes. 'Yes, Hannah,' she said. 'I almost forgot. You must take the babe.'

Astonished, I thought I must have misheard her, so did not reply.

'I promised Mrs Beauchurch, my mistress, that you

would get the babe away if I could not. It is all planned. There is a letter for you . . .' Abby flinched with pain and pressed her hand to her head, then raked it through her hair, knotting a handful of it around her fist as if she would pull it out.

Filled with pity, I waited for the spasm to pass from her before I prompted her to continue. 'A letter?'

She nodded and felt among the folds of her dress for her pocket, then dropped the letter out of the window.

It fell on to the cobblestones and lay there for a moment (for to tell the truth I feared to handle it) until Abby cried that I must take it up. I was forced to do so then, and holding it outstretched before me, I ran home with it.

At the corner I looked back, but Abby had again disappeared.

Chapter Thirteen

The first week of September

'A saddler who had buried all his children dead of the Plague, did desire only to save the life of his remaining little child, and so prevailed to have it received stark naked into the arms of a friend.'

I sobbed all the way back to the shop and people avoided me as I ran, for they probably thought I was afflicted and half-mad.

Sarah was standing in the doorway with a grave expression upon her face, but my sudden tearful appearance distracted her from whatever had caused this. I gave her the letter and explained in a few words about Abby. Without speaking she shut the shop and we went through to our little room in the back.

She turned the letter over in her hands. 'We should steam it over vinegar,' she said.

'But I have already handled it in bringing it here!'

She shrugged, and I knew she was trying not to alarm me. 'Then we won't bother.'

We sat down together on the bed and she peeled up

the seal and opened the folded piece of paper. It was a page torn from a book, the handwriting being on one side.

'It is written in an educated hand,' Sarah said, 'although you can see that whoever it is from—'

'It is from Abby's employer, Mrs Beauchurch,' I said.

'Her hand wavers and she is in some distress.' Sarah then read out the letter, which was addressed to me.

'Dear Hannah,

I beg and beseech you in the name of the Almighty that you take my child, Grace, upon receipt of this letter, and carry her with all speed to my sister the Lady Jane at Highclear House, in Dorchester. My child is lusty and hearty now, but if left in this house of death she will surely perish. There are Certificates of Health for you and your sister, but you must travel under the names of Abigail and myself. A carriage has been procured and will be at the sign of the Eagle and Child in Gracechurch Street each day awaiting your arrival. The driver is my sister's man and has a Certificate to travel.

On reaching Dorchester, Lady Jane will ensure that you and your sister are well cared for. You will be permitted to stay until the Visitation has left London, when you will be given safe passage back.

May the prayers of a mother melt your heart and you find it within yourselves to grant my dying wish and save my child.

By my hand this 30th day of August 1665.

Maria Beauchurch.'

'Abby is terribly sick and so strange that I could scarce believe it was her,' I said to Sarah. I lifted a corner of my skirt and wiped my eyes on it. 'What will we do?'

She put down the letter and turned to look at me. 'We will go, of course,' she said calmly, 'for our own sakes as well as that of the babe. We will not get another chance of leaving London and it grows more dangerous here by the minute.'

I was still shaking from the shock of seeing my poor friend, and from hearing what was asked of us. 'Must we really go?' I asked.

She nodded. 'For when you appeared then, I had just been told a terrible thing by Mr Newbery.'

I looked at her. 'But there are so many terrible things.'

'The Bills. They show six thousand dead in London in the last week.'

'Six thousand!'

'And nearly two more thousand dead of "other causes" – and they fear it will get higher, for there are so many dying all around that there are no longer enough men to board up and guard the houses. Mr Newbery says the afflicted will now begin to walk the streets and infect others, and the whole population may fall.'

I put my face in my hands, uttering a cry of distress. How had I ever thought that living here in this city . . . this charnel house . . . was preferable to living in the serenity I had enjoyed in the country?

Sarah was already moving about our room, pulling things out of our nest of drawers and stuffing them into a cloth bag. 'We will wear our good gowns,' she said. 'For if we are to act the rich mistress and her nursemaid, then we must look the part.'

She stepped out of her workaday dress and apron and threw them on the bed, then took down her best grey taffeta gown and jacket, and put on her little lace hood. ''Tis not the height of fashion,' she said, 'but I daresay that the men at the city gates won't know any better.'

She came to me and clasped my hands in hers. 'This is our way out, Hannah. This will save us!' I did not reply or move and she shook my shoulders gently. 'Set to, Hannah. You can wear your blue and put my little travelling cape over the top.'

I rose and turned so Sarah could unbutton my gown at the back, my mind a mess of thoughts: Tom, Abby, our journey, the babe . . .

'We will shut up the shop and not tell anyone where we're going, for who knows but there might be some law against impersonating a person of quality and using their Certificate of Health,' Sarah said. I nodded obediently. I would let Sarah take charge, for I did not wish to have to decide things myself.

Two bags were packed with some clean shifts and a change of clothes each, and somehow I found myself dressed and ready, a cape around my shoulders and a clean white cap on my head. Sarah decided to leave what there was left of our plague sweetmeats outside the shop for the poor to eat (which they would, of course, immediately) for she said it would just encourage rats if we left them inside.

'And who knows – our sweetmeats might do someone some good,' she said.

There was a knot of fear in my stomach as we

closed our shop behind us. Suppose it was discovered that we were travelling under false documents? Would we then be consigned to the pest hospital (which I had heard was little more than a burial ground)? And – worse still – suppose little Grace carried the plague germs on her? If everyone else in that house had succumbed, why should she be spared?

Sarah secured the door and then, having thought of something else, went back inside and came out carrying a folded linen sheet.

'We mustn't take anything from Abby's house,' she said, pushing the sheet into the bag. 'For they say you should remove nothing from a house which has plague in it.'

'But we are taking Grace—'

'We will have to trust that she is healthy. But she must have no clothing or swaddling cloths on her. Nothing in which plague germs could hide.'

She closed the door again just as Mr Newbery came out from his shop. 'I'm shutting up,' he said. 'What is the point of making parchment and fine writing papers when no one's buying them?' He looked at us curiously. 'But are you shutting up too? I would have thought your business was doing well.'

'We are . . . are . . .' Sarah stumbled.

'Going to church!' I finished for her.

'Well, that's very good and commendable,' Mr Newbery said. 'Though you may not get in through the gates, what with all those corpses lying about!'

'We will somehow manage to get in and pray,' I said piously.

'And spend the rest of the day in silent contemplation of our fate,' Sarah added.

'Well, say a prayer for me,' Mr Newbery said. 'I'll be in a pew in the Three Pigeons.' He gave us a wave and walked off in the opposite direction.

Sarah and I did not speak for some moments, for I was deep in thoughts of what might lie ahead. Deep in thoughts of Tom, too, and as we approached Doctor da Silva's I asked if I might go and say goodbye to him.

'I'd rather you did not,' Sarah said. 'For the less people know about our flight from London, the better.'

'But Tom can be trusted,' I pleaded. 'And think how worried he'll be if he comes down to see me and finds the shop empty. He'll think we've both been taken by the sickness.'

She sighed, but in the end gave me leave to see him. 'Hurry, though,' she said as I pushed open the door of the apothecary's. 'With Abby so very ill, every moment is precious.'

Tom *was* in the shop, and I quickly explained to him and the doctor what was happening, and they were most anxious and concerned for us. The doctor gave me a sleeping draught for the babe, a strong purging elixir for Abby, and also two onions which I was to tell her to roast and place on the buboes to try and bring them to a head. He packed these things into a small valise and told Tom to escort us to Belle Vue House to ensure that we had safe passage.

Any other time I would have been merry whilst walking with Tom through the City, but this was very different. The three of us barely spoke as we hurried along, and when we did it was just to murmur in low tones of the dire things we saw around us. There were more corpses placed outside houses for collection – I saw at least three – and other sad sights: a woman sobbing, 'Dead, all dead!' from a top-floor window and a man dressed only with a rag around his private parts, crying aloud and tearing at his flesh with his fingernails so that his arms and chest ran with blood. We also saw a death cart trundling along, so over-full with corpses that some were slumped across the bench seat with the driver.

Tom hurried us past all these sights until we arrived in the vicinity of Belle Vue House, and here the streets became quieter, most of the residents having gone into the country some time before.

Going round to the back of the house my heart was heavy, for I was fearful of what condition Abby would be in. If she was well I feared the effect giving the babe away would have on her, for she loved Grace, and caring for her gave her something to live for. If she was worse – well, I did not dare think on that.

As before, there was no answer to my call. We all tried, calling softly at first and then more loudly, and in the end Tom gave a most piercing whistle, like a blackbird, but even this did not bring her to the window.

'I fear she may have fallen into a deep sleep,' I said. For I had heard that this is what happened just before plague sufferers died.

'I fear she—' Tom began, but then glanced at me and did not finish.

We looked around us. A large green and gold vine encircled the house, going right up to the fourth floor, but Sarah decided that it was not strong enough to climb, or Tom might have shinned up it.

We called some more but then had to stop, because the watchman on duty at the front of the house came round wanting to know what we were at. Tom, luckily, having been warned of the man's arrival by the sound of his boots on the cobblestones, ducked into one of the empty stables and so was not seen by him.

'Our sister is the maid in this house and we are concerned for her welfare,' I informed the guard – but very politely, for I knew we must not arouse his suspicions or enmity.

'When did you last take in food to anyone in there?' Sarah asked anxiously.

'The milch-ass called this morning as usual and a flagon of milk was sent up,' he said. He looked suspiciously at our bundles of clothes on the ground. 'Anything which goes into this house must go through me. And nothing must come out!'

We assured him that of course it would not, and he went back to the front of the house again.

Tom reappeared. 'I have an idea,' he said. 'As this looks to be a slow business, why don't you go to the Eagle and Child and secure the carriage, while I wait here for you. I will call Abby meantimes, and when you return, if I have not roused her, I will insist on being let in the house. I will say I am an apothecary and that I have been sent by the parish.'

'We cannot ask you to do—' Sarah began, but Tom hushed her.

'Go and get the carriage,' he said. 'You must act with all haste.'

Sarah knew the Eagle and Child, which was a large and notable inn in Gracechurch Street with stables at the back. While Sarah waited in the courtyard, I went in to ask for the inn-keeper's wife and, when she appeared, informed her that I was the maid at Belle Vue House and that my mistress was Mrs Beauchurch.

'Do you have something for us?' I asked.

She was obviously expecting me and, nodding her head, she went to a locked cupboard and took a roll of parchment from it. She then fetched a deep canvas bag. Unrolling the parchment I found it contained a sum of money and the two Health Certificates of which Abby had spoken, one in her name and one in that of Mrs Beauchurch. They stated that, being free of the pestilence we should be granted safe passage out of London. They were signed by the Lord Mayor himself, Sir John Lawrence.

In the canvas bag there was a soft white woollen shawl for Grace, a flask of wine, a travelling rug and cushions for Sarah and myself, also some kid gloves, a lantern and some other little items for our comfort during the journey.

I went outside to the courtyard and rejoined Sarah, and in a few moments two horses were brought out of the stables, and a groom had wheeled out a small blue-varnished carriage, a coat of arms on its door, from the coach house. While we waited there a boy ran helter-skelter through the yard, and returned a few moments later with a stout and bald man of perhaps fifty years. This fellow bowed and introduced himself to us as Mr Carter, coachman to the Lady Jane.

Sarah, holding her head high, told him that she was Mrs Beauchurch.

'Indeed,' he said, giving a slight wink. 'And you are hardly changed since your last visit to Dorchester.'

Sarah inclined her head, and managed very well not

to look askance at this.

'I have been expecting you, and I am to be your coachman and your guard for the journey,' Mr Carter went on. 'Your passage has been considered and your stops planned ahead of us. I only hope you will not find the journey too arduous.'

Sarah, in her role as gracious lady, smiled her thanks. 'We are looking forward to it,' she said, and then hesitated. 'When we are all prepared here, I have to go back to my house to collect my child,' she added. 'It is just a short distance away.'

'I am at your service,' Mr Carter murmured.

As the horses were bridled and prepared I was still in an agony of fear about Abby, but could not help but marvel at the smooth way everything had been made ready for us. Sarah said to me quietly that it was all to do with money, and that anything, any service, could be procured if someone was willing to pay enough for it.

Feeling very nervous, but also very grand – for neither of us had ever been driven in a carriage before – Sarah directed Mr Carter to Belle Vue House. On drawing close by, we asked him to stop just out of view of the courtyard, for we were both anxious about being noticed by the watchman. If this happened, Sarah said, if it became known that we were stealing a child away from an enclosed house, then he would certainly lock us all into the house and inform the magistrates.

Alighting and going to the courtyard, we found that Tom had not been able to rouse Abby, and that he now proposed to go inside the house. 'For what could be more natural than an apothecary should attend his patient,' he said, holding up his valise. 'Doctor da Silva does it all the time.'

'I don't think you should go,' I said worriedly, but although part of me wanted to beg him not to risk such danger, I had no idea how we would secure little Grace otherwise.

Tom took my hand. 'It's nothing. I see plague sufferers every day of the week. Just wish me well and wait here for me.'

'Be careful,' was all I could say in return, and though I knew that these words sounded pitifully inadequate, my mind was so full of fear and dread that I could not think of any others.

While Sarah and I waited, Tom went around to the front of the house. I do not know what he said to the guard, but a few moments later his face appeared at the first-floor window we had been calling up to for so long.

'Is it all right?' I asked breathlessly. 'Have you found Abby?'

He did not reply and I asked again, already knowing in my heart what he was about to say.

'I have,' he said gravely.

Sarah took my hand and held it.

'She is here on the stairs,' he went on, 'but, Hannah, I do not think she suffered much, for there is a look of hope on her face.'

'Her hope was that you would come back,' Sarah said, looking at me with great pity. 'She must have been looking out for you.'

So Abby was dead.

Dead. The word struck me cold and brutal, and the image which came into my head of my lovely friend being no more than a heap of rotting flesh made me want to scream and sob and pull at my clothes like the mad people in the streets did. I dared not indulge myself, though, for we had much to do if I was to carry out Abby's last wishes. I did not even allow myself to weep, but knew I must put my feelings to one side until later.

'What . . . what of the babe?' I asked Tom, and I was bitterly scared now, for if she too was dead, then all this had been for nothing.

Tom disappeared, and came back a moment later with a bundle in his arms. 'I have her here,' he said, holding up Grace. 'She was sleeping, but now she smiles at me.'

At this I felt a rush of tears to my eyes. 'Is she well?' I asked anxiously.

'She seems well enough,' Tom said, looking her over. 'I am no expert but her eyes are bright, she seems well-fed, and she is pink-cheeked.'

'Will you bring her out to us now?' Sarah asked in a low voice.

'And risk being seen by the guard?' Tom said. 'I think not. We must—'

'Is there a basket nearby?' I asked suddenly. 'There was one with a rope attached which the household used to get its provisions.'

'There is,' Tom said, bending down for it. 'And I think it will be just big enough.'

'Will you take off her things, Tom,' Sarah said. 'We have brought a clean sheet to wrap her in.'

Tom disappeared for a moment or two to do this, and while he was out of view my mind was a perfect whirlpool of fear. He then reappeared with Grace naked within the basket. Lifting this into the air, he tested the rope that held it, and then Sarah and I stood with arms outstretched as he carefully lowered the precious bundle to the ground.

I took little Grace out – and indeed she did look healthy, with plump pink limbs and a fine head of hair – and as we wrapped her in the clean sheet she looked so pretty and innocent that Sarah and I both fell to weeping at her sad destiny in being orphaned so young.

Tom, watching from above, asked us what the matter was. 'Have you seen some mark on her body?' he said anxiously.

I shook my head. 'We are just weeping for . . .' I began, but found I could not explain why.

'For the sadness of the occasion,' Sarah finished with a sigh.

Tom said he was mighty relieved that the babe was well and had no marks on her, and told us that he had a mind to remove Abby's corpse from the stairs, and not leave it in such disarray. He disappeared to do this, but a moment later, to our great horror, we heard a shout inside the house, and the face of the watchman appeared at the same window.

'What mischief are you doing?' he yelled to us. And then he saw the basket and the rope, and Grace in my arms, and began roaring at us to stop, saying he would call the magistrates and have us locked up as kidnappers and common thieves.

We were in a terrible confusion then, for we did not know what to do for the best. I felt that we could not just run off leaving Tom in the plague-torn house, for it would be known that he'd had a part in our stealing of Grace.

Sarah picked up our bundles and pulled my arm, though. 'We must go! If we want to get away, we must go now!'

And I knew she was right. Holding the babe tightly, cradling her head, I began to run with Sarah towards our coach. Mr Carter was still sitting atop in the driver's seat, and reaching it, Sarah opened the door and clambered in, then turned to take Grace from me.

Panting and shaking with fright, I handed the babe to her. I then climbed in myself as quickly as I was able, calling to Mr Carter to drive off with all speed.

As we started off and the carriage turned into the main street, my attention was caught by a blur of movement as Tom came running from the house, sprinted across the roadway and arrived on the corner just as our horses galloped past him.

We had time for just one thing: to blow a kiss to each other.

I leaned forward in my seat, trying to see Tom until the last possible moment, and in this way saw the watchman run out of the house and stare after our coach. Tom ran off, and it looked as if the watchman was hesitating, wondering whether to go after him. He chose us to chase, however, and began to run down the centre of the road ringing a bell and shouting.

This did not alarm us unduly, for within no time at all the horses had gathered speed and we had left him behind. We were going at a goodly pace now, swaying and bumping on the uneven cobbles, and found we had to sit well back, bracing our legs, to enable us to keep our positions. We sat on opposite seats, gazing at each other in a mixture of excitement and fear.

'Close the curtains,' Sarah said. 'A lady and her maid would not allow the common people to gaze in on them.'

I did so, then begged Sarah to let me hold Grace. Smiling, we had a small dispute about who should nurse her, but Sarah at last agreed that it would be more usual for the babe to be held by the maid rather than the lady, and passed her to me. Grace was quiet, the movement of the carriage having almost sent her off to sleep again.

We galloped and jolted through the streets, twisting and turning down narrow passageways, and found out later that Mr Carter had taken us a complex way around in case the watchman found means to follow us. Peeping through a crack in the curtain, I saw few passers-by, and none who looked at us with any interest, for people were very much keeping within their houses now and only going out to buy what food was necessary to keep them alive. After some minutes of fast, jolting driving, we heard Mr Carter shout at the horses and rein them in. They fell into a walk.

Sarah pulled the curtain to one side. 'Mr Carter,' she said, 'can you not maintain the speed?'

'I can, Ma'am,' he said, 'but we are approaching the gate on London Bridge and I do not think it meet that we should arrive there all of a hugger-mugger.'

'No. Indeed!' Sarah said hastily, and she sank back once more on to her seat. We shared an anxious glance and composed ourselves as best we could.

After a moment we heard a 'Whoa!' from Mr Carter and the carriage came to a standstill.

'Be calm, Hannah,' Sarah said quietly. 'Remember that everything depends on us being who our

Certificates say we are.'

I nodded but could not reply, for my throat felt tight and constricted. I put out a finger and stroked little Grace's cheek, praying that things would go well.

Mr Carter was hailed by a rough-sounding voice and someone asked his business. In reply, we heard him explain that he was taking a lady of high breeding to stay with her sister in the country. 'As she has a new-born infant, I wish to make good time and proceed with speed,' he finished.

The curtain was then pulled aside and a dishevelled, bearded fellow looked in on us. He carried a blunderbuss in his hand and did not look as if he'd hesitate to use it.

'Your name?' he asked bluntly.

'I am Mistress Beauchurch,' Sarah replied haughtily. 'My infant daughter is Grace Beauchurch and my maid here is Abigail Palmer.'

'Your certificates to travel?' the fellow asked, and Sarah drew our passes from the canvas bag and handed them over.

'Is there not one for the child?'

Sarah shook her head. 'She is but newly-born. We were told she wouldn't require one.'

His brawny hand plucked at the covering which held Grace and as he looked at her, frowning, I was thankful that Grace was small for her weeks, and that the fellow apparently did not know what size a new-born child should have been.

Losing interest in Grace, he held our certificates up to the light. 'There have been forgeries.'

'Those are no forgeries,' Sarah said with spirit. 'Sir John signed these himself in my presence.'

The fellow spat on them, then rubbed at the ink signature with a grimy finger until it smudged. He thrust them back at Sarah, looking her up and down searchingly.

'And you are Mistress Beauchurch, are you?'

'I am,' Sarah's voice rang out like a true aristocrat and I looked at her admiringly.

'First lady I've seen with rough hands,' the man said. 'Looks more like you've been in charge of the washhouse.'

Sarah looked at him witheringly. 'My good man,' she said, 'the plague is rife and most of my servants are fled. A lady must learn to fend for herself – and besides, I do not trust anyone except myself to wash and tend to my precious child's needs.'

The man gave a bitter laugh. 'Oh, 'tis right, the plague is a great leveller. Even a great lady has to stoop to the washtub nowadays.' He still did not move out of the roadway, but stood there looking at us through narrowed eyes. I felt a cold trickle of sweat begin its journey down my back and was mighty scared.

He brought his face to the carriage window. 'Would you risk anything to get out of London?' he asked.

'I don't . . . I don't know what you mean,' Sarah said.

'What is it worth to you, lady?'

Sarah quivered. 'How dare you!' she said. 'I should have you birched for such impudence.'

'Call the other guard, then, if you've a mind to,' the fellow said easily. 'He'd be interested to see someone like you – someone who is only play-acting a fine lady. There are strict laws against what you're doing.'

Sarah was transfixed and I could not contain a gasp of horror. Did he actually know something, or was he just trying his luck?

'Although, if you were to grease my palm a little—'

'Wh . . . what?' Sarah faltered.

'He wants money!' Mr Carter barked from above. 'Give him what you have and let's be on our way.'

Sarah started, then rummaged in the canvas holdall for the little bag of gold coins we'd been given. Taking out three of these, she thrust them at the fellow.

He looked at the coins, then at us. He seemed astounded, but still he did not move. Panicking now, not really knowing whether what had been given was enough, I snatched the bag from Sarah and pushed another two gold angels into his palm.

'Drive on!' I called to Mr Carter, and as he whipped up the horses the fellow staggered back, staring at the coins he held as if they were stars fallen from the skies.

'We gave him far too much!' Sarah said as we galloped across London Bridge.

'Never mind!' I said. 'We're on our way.'

Leaning forward slightly, I pulled back the curtains a little so I could see out. We had crossed the bridge now – that same London Bridge I had approached with such anticipation and excitement only a few months before. The traitors' heads were still there on their spikes over the gateway, but I also saw the desolate sight of a newly-hung corpse, a man who – no doubt having contracted the sickness and despairing – had made away with himself.

How green I'd been when I'd arrived. I knew now that it was not only cut-throats and villains that one should be wary of in London, but something far more deadly, something unseen and altogether more terrible.

I looked down at the face of little Grace and breathed out a sigh. She must live on, for her survival was all I could do for Abby.

Abby. My friend. I would think about her later, and would earnestly try to think of the sunny, joyful girl who'd been my sweet companion, and not the pitiful wraith I'd last seen at the window.

I leaned against Sarah for comfort and her head inclined towards mine. We were well on the road now, and I felt we would reach Dorchester and survive, for we had not come this far to be overtaken by man or plague. London would survive, too, and I would return to it, and to Tom, and I knew I would not die unkissed.

Glossary

atonement being in harmony with God, from the 16th-century phrase *at onement*.

cabalistic sign a sign used in a secret or occult doctrine or science.

cambric a fine white linen or cotton fabric.

charnel deathlike.

charnel house a building or vault in which bones or corpses are kept.

cony rabbit.

cutpurse a thief or pickpocket who stole by cutting the drawstrings of money purses.

electuary a purgative medicine mixed with honey or sugar syrup in some sweet confection.

fustian a hard-wearing fabric with short velvety nap (pile); made of twilled cotton, or cotton mixed with linen or wool.

groundlings those who stood on the ground, the cheapest part of a playhouse, to watch a theatrical performance.

haberdashery small items for the dressmaker, such as ribbons, laces and silks, as well as hats and caps, and fabric articles for the household.

halberd a weapon which combined a spear and battleaxe on a pole of up to about two metres in length.

marchpane an archaic word for marzipan, the main ingredients of which are ground almonds and sugar.

meet an archaic word meaning proper, fitting, or correct.

milch-ass an ass, or donkey, whose milk was sold by its owner.

patch Through the 17th and 18th centuries fashionable men and women wore patches, like beauty spots, on their face and/or visible parts of the upper body to make them look more attractive and often to cover blemishes.

patten a wooden-soled over-shoe raised up on a circular metal frame and worn to keep one's shoes and long skirts above the muck on the ground.

periwig In the 1660s, a periwig of false hair hanging in curls from a central parting was an essential part of a fashionable man's attire and often disguised a lack of his own hair.

pesthouse a hospital that cared for people with an infectious disease.

poultice a moist and often heated mixture of substances applied to sore or inflamed parts of the body to improve blood circulation and reduce inflammation.

Puritan In the 16th and 17th centuries the more extreme English Protestants aimed to purify the Church of England of most of its ceremony and other aspects they deemed to be Catholic. Adhering to strict moral and religious principles, the Puritans were opposed to luxury and sensual enjoyment.

quarantine enforced isolation, usually of people and animals who have an infectious disease or who may be carriers of it.

swaddle In the 16th century it was thought beneficial to swaddle a new-born baby by wrapping it tightly in linen or other cloth.

worsted a fabric with a hard, smooth, close-textured surface, made from a closely twisted woollen yarn.

Notes on London's Plague, 1665

All the quotations at the chapter headings are from Pepys's *Diary*, which I used for background information. I also used a book published in 1926 called *The Great Plague of London* by W. G. Bell, where I found most of the stories of ordinary people. *Restoration London* by Liza Picard was also invaluable. The idea for Sarah's sweetmeat shop came to me when I read in seventeenth-century Court Records a young girl's answer to the question of what she did for a living: 'I make sweetmeats and chocolett cakes for persons of quality and gentlemen's houses . . .'

During September, after Hannah and Sarah had left London, the numbers of people dying of plague continued to rise. Over 8,000 people died every week in September. Following this, as the weather became colder, the numbers on the Bills of Mortality slowly began to fall. The end of the Great Plague was at last in sight. By the following February, the city was deemed to be free enough of plague for the king and his court to return.

Although London was far and away the largest city in Britain, it was small compared to the size it is now. It is thought that about 300,000 people lived in it – and that one third of those (that is, more than 100,000) perished during the Great Plague. Most of these were the poor, who could not get away from the city.

Accounts have been found for the killing of as many

as 4,380 dogs in the city alone and probably three times as many cats. This was, of course, misguided, because the animals may have been controlling the very vermin that are thought to have spread the plague.

Nell Gwyn, the orange seller who rose to become a mistress to King Charles II, was fifteen in 1665. She is depicted in records as merry, witty and lovable as well as strikingly attractive. Pepys was an admirer, referring to her as 'pretty, witty Nelly'.

The plague was a terrifying and mystifying disease and people were prepared to try anything to avoid catching it. Everyone was very superstitious – even Pepys carried a 'lucky rabbit's foot' in his pocket. People saw what they thought were portents of death in the form the clouds took, or in natural but inexplicable phenomena like comets. They sometimes carried a piece of paper with the word ABRACADABRA written in a triangle, thus:

A
AB
ABR
ABRA
ABRAC
ABRACA
ABRACAD
ABRACADA
ABRACADAB
ABRACADABR
ABRACADABRA

They took all the conconctions mentioned in this book and many more. One of these recipes begins: 'Take black snails and cut and gash them with your knife, then take the liquor which comes from them and add it to a goodly quantity of wine . . .' It was also thought to be beneficial to drink your medicine from a hanged man's skull.

It is now known that the plague was spread by rat fleas carrying the plague bacilli and jumping from their hosts, the rats, to humans. The bacilli attacked the body's lymphatic system, causing inflamed and painful swellings in the lymph glands, called 'buboes'. No one knows exactly why or how it died out, but bubonic plague never again hit this country quite as badly as it did in 1665. It was feared that it would return as the weather grew warmer in 1666, but it did not, and although the rest of the country was hit, London remained relatively free of the plague. On 2 September, 1666, however, another terrible disaster occurred: The Great Fire.

Recipes from
the Seventeenth Century

Sugared plums

Sugared orange peel

Candied angelica

Marchpane fruits

Frosted rose petals

Sugared plums

Place about twelve firm, pitted plums in sufficient water to cover and cook gently until just tender. Strain the liquid, keep back about half a pint in a jug and add 6 oz sugar. Boil this up and pour over fruit.

Leave for two days, then drain off water into a saucepan and add another two ounces of sugar. Boil up and pour over fruit.

Repeat this process every day for eight to twelve days, until the liquid is as thick as honey. Leave the plums soaking in this for a further three to ten days, according to how sweet you want them to be.

Remove and place the plums in a very low oven or airing cupboard until thoroughly dry, then dip each fruit quickly into boiling water, drain off excess moisture and roll in caster sugar. Pack in greaseproof paper until needed.

Sugared orange peel

Wash two large unwaxed oranges, and use a small sharp knife to cut off the tops and bottoms. Slice off the peel very thinly, from top to bottom, taking care to get only the zest. Cut the zest into long neat strips, then cut it in half, so that each strip is about 4 x 1 cm. Boil a saucepan of water, add the orange peel and boil for three minutes. Drain and plunge the peel into cold water. Repeat this blanching process twice more, using fresh boiling water each time.

Put 500ml of cold water and 500g caster sugar into a saucepan and boil until the sugar is dissolved. Add the drained peel and simmer for one hour. Drain and dry on a rack for three hours.

Candied angelica

Cut several tender angelica stems into equal lengths, cover with water and boil for five minutes. Peel off the outer skin and simmer until the stems turn light green. Drain and dry on a cooling rack. Cover with plenty of sugar and leave for three days. Then place in water and simmer gently until they turn green again. Drain, roll in caster sugar and dry on a rack.

Marchpane (Marzipan) fruits (A modern-day version)

450g ground almonds
225g icing sugar
225g caster sugar
2 eggs
1 tbs. lemon juice

Whisk the eggs and lemon juice. Stir in the sugars and ground almonds, and use your hands to form the mixture into a ball.

Divide this ball up according to how many different fruits you intend to make, and knead a few drops of colouring agent into each new ball.

Make up your fruits by shaping as necessary, and refrigerate until needed.

Frosted rose petals

Break apart full pink or red roses and remove the white bottom edge of each petal. Sprinkle the petals with rose water (or dip them in a bowl of it) then lay them to dry on kitchen paper in the sunshine. Sift icing sugar over them. Every two hours or so, repeat the process, turning them over each time, until the petals have dried to a crisp. Lay in boxes between white paper.